Deliberations in

DUNG

It's

A Beetle's Life

of Excrementism and Humanism

André Buitendag

Contents

Prologue

In *this* beginning the heaven and the earth are already created. And the earth has formed rocky outcrops where there is life even in the darkness on the face of a once-deep granite plateau, exposed and worn by ages of tropical rainwater flowing across the savanna grasslands into the River Mubundovi. On its meander across the landscape, the river touches lives, and passes farms and villages; in summer gushing after each of the frequent rainstorms, and in winter drying patchily into muddy holes, or simply coming to a standstill as a murky pool.

There is a stillness over the veld; and over the rocky outcrops, the lichen-mottled clumps of grey stones that appear harsh and desolate in the scrubby surrounds. You could amble around any one of them and hardly notice how much life is passing you by, until your eye catches a rainbow lizard twitching its neck as it bakes on a flat rock-chip, or trapdoor spiders darting between the threads of webs spiraling into gaping holes, and rock rabbits peeping up in spaces a darting distance from their burrows. There are scorpions under those rocks, and passages and labyrinths swarming with ants sheltered from the glare of the African sun. And on parching afternoons when the breeze is blowing elsewhere, when all seems at rest, the freshest dassie droppings are reminders that nature can be serene and still, but is never stagnant.

Dassies, innately aggressive and not infrequently violent, scamper on the perpetual search for anything greenish and growing. These hyraxes, or rock rabbits as they are sometimes called, are veld survivors, and will eat plants that are too aromatic for, or toxic to, other creatures. But even they need to avoid the poisoned grain left by the rifle-toting farmers, and their blundering hounds. In turn, their droppings will be the pellets that provide sustenance and shelter for a myriad of insects.

Observe these newly-paired beetles rolling a dung-ball in which the female will lay an egg. But first they must scuttle it to a safe spot: here, next to some others, it is half-buried on the shady side of a stony sheath where, if conditions are aligned, and the bundu permits, it should soon hatch. Is it conceivable that a creature whose life begins pressed up against a small boulder, a mere dung-beetle's flight away from the river, could make it through countless and contrasting experiences in this confusion of conflicting worlds?

Nearby browses a sprightly pair of grey duikers. They blink and nibble distractedly at a sour-plum shrub that could, in seasons to come, grow taller than the surrounding anthills and offer them cover and protection. The buck nudges and nips, playfully, and horns the nearby bushes, and wets them. Is this the beginning of their courtship? In her delicate struttings, the doe surely knows. As long as there remains the vegetation from which to draw water, this seems a good place for them to loiter, and there will be no need to browse riverwards risking encounters with the dangers that lurk there. There are also, plentiful in the summer veld, fruits and tubers, insects and even small birds or mammals on which to feed. Venturing to the fringes of human settlement, to the lush gardens of a nearby village or farmyard is sometimes safe at night but, for lingering, the open savanna stillness is the place of choice.

The quiet of nature is not 'silence', for that is a human construct, like their buildings and carved roads and wild dust-spewing vehicles, and is unlike the daily rising and setting of the sun or the phases of the moon. Or the displays of the Milky Way at night, or the fatiguing heat of summer and the biting chill of winter. There is no right time – there is just savanna stillness and, like a rolling, tumbling dung-ball, time passing – for that is where the peace that gives life begins. For that is where enlightenment begins.

Chapter 1: Egg

Call me *Catharsius*. That places me in a broad and vague enough order. It calls out to a life of growing and shedding, and moving on. It's suited to me at any time. At any stage it will classify me. But names are only given when beginnings start to have meaning: humans presume this, don't they? So am I to remain nameless, naturally? Call me stubborn.

This was all before I became a creature of value and of deserving, and before I began to roll. When I learnt to purposefully move manure, to toil, then, and only after this emergence, was I 'Rollo'. But time isn't a dung-ball to be pushed backwards. Discernment invites revisiting the moments of peace that begin life.

I was an egg once. Once. More than – or so my feelers sense – one entire revolution of the savanna ago. Preceding me, the veld had yielded a pair of dung-beetles, whose dust-trails crossed, and they met, and settled their suitability in chemical agreement. Then they toiled, and created an orb of moist excrement, and laboured to lodge it between a rock and a hyrax burrow.

It was semi-submerged by their other dung-balls, and formed a kind of nest-pile that was not too wet and not too dry. This was my first of many habitats, a half-buried home, the brood-ball into which I was laid. There were siblings in similar coverings around and above me as I was developing, on the edge, and relatively lower. In the vigilance that nature bestows, my parents kept numerous eyes on all the balls. Seasons of growth have since circulated for me to be in my place, able to look back, and sense the simple wisdom – is that what instinct is? – dung-beetle parents have, to not put all their eggs in one brood-ball, and to know what balls it takes to breed.

That's because not every ball hits. Squelchy, white insect eggs are nutritious, a perfect mouthful for prowling, marauding ants and swooping, pecking birds. For only a few rotations of the earth under the savanna sun, we remained fixed in the veld, and motionless in manure – or as still as moist growth permits. In the dry and often desolate bundu, dung-beetle *zai* were sought-after, and looked-after. And I was kept innocently safe, in a protecting brood-ball: parental care extended deep into dung.

Chapter 2: Larva

With effort, a great escape is possible. If that exertion entails biting and involves wriggling – even thrusting, a breakout can be rendered probable. Locating gaps and opportunities in the receding egg-skin is a dung-beetle larva's first challenge on the arduous journey towards breaking the surface, to life on, and no longer in, the earth.

I knew, even then, that when the skin of an egg has outperformed its purpose, as mine had, if you devour it, you can be *it*. You can reach up and claim the prize of a mighty metamorphosis in manure. It *is* every day that you should eat as much as you can. If you've just hatched, your all-consuming job is to feed. And digest, I did!

Dung-beetle larvae are endowed with massive mandibles, installments for this gustatory investment, this gathering of energy, this stuffing, that will serve and nourish a lifetime. Hardened and tooth-like, these mouthparts outclass and outperform the flanking antenna, and where adults stick to liquids, the voracious larvae gorge on solid dung with their mega-, multi-purpose mandibles.

I could sense my mother communicating to me. She was connecting from above, and sharing, in short but assured scrapes of meaning. And I'd respond – ridiculous raspings at first, but baby-rubs are beginnings that make sounds in the stillness. There were other vibrations and rustlings too, sibling brood-balls around and above, scratching in growth, and growing in response. These were beetle-care beginnings, and maternal instincts and impulses kept her counting her larvae until they were hatched.

A father, I never sensed. There were no paternal patterings passed down. Perhaps he'd rolled on, and unearthed a better breeder somewhere else. Maybe he found other mates, and other opportunities, as males often do. Perhaps he'd been threatened, and thrown, and overturned in a struggle, and had scurried away. All that's known is that there's no cowardice in insects, only self-preservation.

Larval life is not all festive feasting, however. Development in the savanna can depend on how dry or sandy or clayish the earth is, or how much water it holds, or how deep the brood-balls are buried, or what they are comprised of. There are always conditions. Always. Conditions and contrasts in all ways. A well-rolled and shielded brood-ball (preferably of the diverse-microorganism faeces of omnivores: duiker-droppings will certainly serve!) holds its moisture when the rays of the sun are pounding the outcrops, and stays saturated when the clouds are whisked away by sweltering breezes. But when the summer rains fall without cessation, and the veld is flooded and the soil is clogged, the young drown in the mud.

Not being the strongest egg, and a later larval developer, I was lucky, conditions kept me alive. My bundu-balance had begun before my birth. I, Mhezi the Larva, had my ball *and* ate it! Without the need to compete for food, as I guzzled and grew and swelled my spiracles and needed more room, I shed the outer coverings that contained my bloating body. Ecdysis exits ensued. Like the changes of a moon, I grew from slight and bowed, in molting instar stages, as many times as beetles have legs, to full and round.

In the repetitions of early life, preparations make perfect. And developed larvae know that dung is the sweat of super-bugs. To maintain a complete and protected chamber, I toiled against my brood-ball filling with (my own) inedible frass. I was careful always to keep mandibles-up at the head of the ball, and labored unceasingly to keep its interior sealed with my own poop. Until, chamber-chomping complete, laid-back, face-aloft and supine-set, I readied myself for the most significant challenge to stillness known, intuitively only, in the world of bug-ery.

Chapter 3: Pupa

It will be the stillest of times, it will be the busiest of times, it will be the age of insight, it will be the age of incomprehension, it will be the epoch of containment, it will be the epoch of release, it will be the season of light, it will be the season in darkness, it will be the spring of hope, it will be the winter of waiting; Catharsius has beetledom before him, Mhezi has frass below him; all siblings in the outcrop are metamorphosing towards the Milky Way, some will become beetles, some will perish as pupae.

The complete pupation will take less than a month, and just as the moon advances in another cycle of phases, life on the veld follows. While appearing as a semi-hardened mass with a protective shell, the pupa transmutes from a squishy, chubby mass as it digests itself from the inside. Its body is broken down into undifferentiated cells, which then, regulated by hormones, differentiate into the cells needed for the formation of beetle eyes, wings, legs, internal reproductive organs and external genitalia, and adult sensory organs.

Developing pupae are unable to breathe as they moult, and as the exuviae are outgrown and shed, and the next instar or developmental stage ensues. They rest in hollow shells now, tiny spikes on their backs to raise themselves clear of the surface that they are reaching towards but which, at this stage, may contain fungi that infect, and kill. It is, like the egg-phase, a period of helplessness and passivity. It is a sedentary time of imposed inaction, of independence over which there is no control. It is incarceration in the savanna, a forced lockdown, and the release, when it comes, will be an earth-moving breakout.

My mother's care and communications continued unabated despite the stillness from me inside the brood-ball. Her mouthparts seldom stopped their scrapings, and the rubbings of her legs against her body were incomprehensible to me in the motionlessness of mine still in formation.

Unexpectedly, a savanna wind picked up. It blew in snappy gusts as clouds choked the rays of the sun. The duikers edged into the patchy protection of a nearby acacia, and dassies popped their heads up, alerted, to see what on earth was happening. Earlier that hot season, there had been days of unusual coolness, reflections perhaps of more widespread, global fluctuations. More serious and destructive repercussions were being felt everywhere; there were strange storms at sea, dubious droughts on land, and temperatures higher and lower and more variable than last year's record extremes. It was as though the weather was issuing warnings, and climates were in change.

For the pupae on the rocky outcrops near the River Mubundovi, cooler times were a blessing: proportions of dung-beetle larvae that grow into adulthood are greatly improved by a cold period, especially in the third larval stage. The milder conditions lowered the soil temperature, and stimulated and enhanced brood-ball development. But the biting, drawn-out winter, the icy season when progress in the veld is formative, and not entirely stilled, was approaching.

Mhezi, the larva, finding more of himself as Catharsius, a coprophage, had outgrown his brood-ball boundaries. His underground metamorphosis was accomplished, and his earthly role of 'purifier' beckoned boldly. In the savanna, where nothing ever comes from nothing, survival starts in stillness. And with time spent in imposed immobility, his urge to activate was triggered. He would begin his second stage of insect activity, by emerging.

Chapter 4: Becoming

As Mhezi the larva awoke one morning from a series of unsettling expansions, he found himself transformed in his brood-ball into a complete insect. He lay on his furrowed back and saw, with newly-formed compound eyes, as he lifted his head up a little, his arched abdomen divided up into rigid bow-like sections. His numerous legs, comparatively thin and in connection to the rest of his circumference, flickered helplessly, as they rested on clammy and closed pairs of wings.

Could he really grasp what had happened to him? Although he had lived through an unusually extended number of days in the pupal chamber of preparation, that natural stillness was not 'patience', for it too, like 'silence', is a human construct. He was held in quiet quarantine, where he had managed to maintain a constant and sufferably high temperature, which now fired him towards the surface, and he emerged.

As a larva with only a few simple eyes on each side of his head, he had needed and so enjoyed limited vision.

He was protected from perceptiveness. But now, with well-developed crystalline cones, and orthogonally-organised rhabdom microvilli, and thousands of hexagonal lenses, as well as a discernible clearzone: what fresh insights could be gained. What new worlds and galaxies could be observed, and grasped.

What incredible body segments I'd grown! From the confines of my cuticle I'd sprouted an outstanding pair of antenna. I'd formed first and second maxillae. I'd fashioned first, second and third legs with the corresponding extremities of tarsi connected to the tibiae connected to the femora connected to the trochanters connected to the coxae connected to the three segments of my thorax! It seemed clearer than ever that I was uncovering the ways of a beckoning future. I was unearthing the many trails down which I'd soon scutter.

And, not to boast unnecessarily, because insects are only forced to show off when they're threatened, or need to assert dominance, or survive as the fittest: my superb scutellum – and not to forget my genital sclerites – was to prove substantially more than adequate. Time would reveal. Though at this stage my gonads were still to mature – in more than one way I was a late-developer, from half-hidden-buried to now semi-fully-formed – my parameres were in studly shape and would, also when circumstances ripened, elongate into genital claspers. My three-dimensional aedeagus would prove perfectly proficient at streaming sperm from its currently-concealed internal sac which I could and would turn inside out when so *so* enticed. Gone were all those sapping thoughts of life as an underappreciated outsider. Things certainly were looking good – and good-looking.

But big questions remained. Would all this make me a dung-beetle tumbler or a tunneller or a dweller? I noticed front legs marvellously modified for a lifestyle of dung-digging but, and despite the sun rising, unnoticed, wasn't insightful enough then to know that I'd already been designed. I was made to be a tumbler, and to roll that way. It dawned on me: I wasn't meant to be a mere dirt-digger. I was destined to topple and tumble and turn, and ride, high on dung-balls. I knew what I had always been, and was becoming aware then of what I was, and would always be: a *detritis-digesting, crap-consuming coprophagous dung-beetle*!

Chapter 5: Emerging

The earth moved. For me! There was a tumultuous transfer of topsoil. I shattered the surface. It was a grand moment, indeed. Never was there such an almighty explosion announcing the uproar that gave life, to *me*. Surely somewhere there was a lightning flash, a thud of thunder, or some volcanic vibration heralding my drama in dung!

The Big Bang.

The earth hardly moved, or noticed, the little loosening of loam and parting of particles that lightly scratched the earth's surface. It was a granule moment, a jiffy adjustment. Often in the outcrops there are stillnesses that signify the peace that gives life, to countless creatures. Surely, it was a manure murmur, a poo-ping, some simple sideshow in sand.

A petty plop.

In the savanna, distance lends engrossment to the veld. Humidity and humility settle on the ground, to give growth where the bundu teaches, and as the seasons instruct. There are instincts to obey, and concerns to consider; flashbacks to take creatures forward, and *kungufisiza* that leaves them confused.

In time, I'd find new sustenance in older, drier dung-balls. I'd absorb the ways to make them fresh, and I'd learn how to roll – and backwards too. There'd be opportunities to face what it meant to turn and push, to sometimes be on the ball alerted, and at other times disheartened when an uphill battle ended in a downhill roll. I'd eke out an existence constantly considering how I clawed back, and primed my palps, and restarted – repeatedly.

At dusk when the cicada chirpings had crescendoed to screeching, the maternal scratchings intensified, and seemed closer than ever to me in my pupal preparedness. Far above my brood-ball, unseen but somehow sensed, the Milky Way was beaming. Looking back, I grasp that the anticipation, that unrestrained enthusiasm to break free, was greater than the arrival. Thinking ahead, I flinch at my overpitched pronouncements.

I was never filled with the fear of how much effort the emergence would take, or whether I had the beetle-strength to rise on the occasion. In those moments of unfurling feelers, of instinct and of impulse, and a flaring force that was not to be contained, there was no restraint, no coprophage control. I was to be unfettered, delivered from the confines of a crumbling brood-ball through which I'd devoured with mandibles ready to crunch the cosmos. I was a born-again creature, arranged to ascend, fit to fly heavenwards.

On the savanna, there is opportunity in the willingness to wait. The lizard hesitates between head-flicks; the dassie delays to validate its dart underground; and the duiker pauses mid-prance to eat, while on the alert.

I *did* wait – I *did* emerge.

Was there glory in the plop, or only a feeler of some splendor in the anticipation of it? Does coming-out need to be marked by an exaggerated occasion when it is merely a part of a transition? The hidden stillness, the closeted, underground evolution has to burst out. Are the flashes of fierceness and fabulosity not a façade to foil fear? The dread of the unknown, of starting again in a hostile new world, the distress of danger, the oppression of opposition, and the alarm at being eaten, gnaw. Is progress measured by the moment or the outcome?

Chapter 6: Surfacing

The past is a fragmented brood-ball: they do things differently there. I'd consumed the course taking me from underground to openness. I'd endured the going-between that not all insects survive. I was above it all, having moved from the edge, I was back from the brink. I'd ascended from a lower-positioned brood-ball in a place of relative late development, into an overwhelmingly ordure-oriented and faeces-filled new world. I was a second-bester succeeding the first time. No longer Mhezi the larva, I'd risen.

There was no stopping or space, at that stage, for consideration of how much starts in stillness. Then wasn't the time for any more depth or ruminations. I was chomping at the mandibles, and ready to roll. There, posed in every moment of that midday heat, paused a questionably confident coprophagous, fully-formed but still finding my feelers.

And what fine feelers I felt them to be! With all upbeat balls in the air, I scrambled past other grounded and used brood-chambers. The most impressive sibling-sarcophagus was centred under the boulder's overhang, where it would've had the best shade, and the best shield. This last-rolled and finest-of-the-batch brood-ball, now lying discarded and fragmented, had obviously exploded and released a top tumbler. While further out on the edge, where there was no accommodating ball-room, and no protecting ledge or outcrop, lay the crumbled husk of another brood-ball. I sensed it. I recognized that wrapping. And inside was a desiccated, still-born sibling, exposed and dead in the dust-path where a fleeing duiker had, unknowingly, given it its fatal kick in the ball.

It was a still and sweltering afternoon on the savanna. Having just been released from my stifling underground pupae-period, I was ready to be cooler. In the world of scurrying insects, deeds and dealings are determined by surface temperature. Was all of life going to be this horribly hot? Would I warm to the wisdom of dealing with the heat, without burning up? What life-choices would be mine? Would I be an evening insect or a day-time dung-beetle? Or would that, like living as a roller and not a tunneller or a digger, be pre-destined? There is so much that rests in the tarsis-twitchings of fate.

I halted, and inspected my new self. At the beginnings of dung-beetle tarsi there are spikes, and at their ends are claws. For ingesting, I saw sensing palps with which I could touch and taste, and maxillae to manipulate, and a labrum above for intake positioning. But my antenna wavered and waggled. I was gripped in a mental metamorphosis – for the first time. I juddered. As this newfangled contemplation clasped onto disorientation, my femurs flattened, tibias lowered, and my thorax clonked onto the clay.

The savanna has a word for downheartedness: *kungufisiza,* or 'thinking too much'. Down in the mouthparts, overthinking, perplexed and in post-pupaeic panic, I came to rename myself 'Pushover'. Humans give themselves names too, usually for life, but I wasn't hatched to be bound by clumsy labelling for that long. How can any life-form evolve when its label doesn't? I'd only just found my way through a casing of crap, and was a beetle above. After the emergence-elation, and the recovery-reality following the *kungufisiza*-confusion and, burying that fainthearted new name, as sudden as a savanna cloudburst, hunger hit.

Chapter 7: Finding

Dung-beetles are always dabbling in dung. They are always hungry so they are always busy, and so busy that they are always hungry. The savanna has no word for 'over-eating'.

Moments after I emerged, my exploits in excrement ingestion began. Regarding the issues of my faecal-feastings: the fresher, the finer; and the warmer, the worthier. A pile of poop is one place where heat is a plus. In manure, there's tang in temperature, and fulfillment where it's hot. A dried-out dung-patty, like a dead sibling's withered brood-ball, is an opportunity wasted, and isn't palatable to even the pickiest of coprophagi.

Insects are tongueless. With taste buds on their feelers and legs, dung-beetles will turn away their antenna and turn up their tarsi at solid foods. In fact, because they feed on bacteria, fungi and microscopic particles of gut epithelium from the manure-makers, and only tiny fractions of dung, adult dung-beetles are not dung-feeders, or coprophagous, in the strictest sense. Their sense of taste, their gustatory chemoreception, responds most favourably to soggy scat-slurpees. If man's *Bristol Stool Scale* was a menu, dung-beetles' preferred faeces would be *Type 5:* Soft blobs with clear cut edges; *Type 6:* Fluffy pieces with ragged edges, a mushy stool (diarrhoea), or *Type 7:* Watery, no solid pieces, entirely liquid (diarrhoea). Irritable Bowel Syndrome would be the *pièce de résistance.*

Dung-beetles are diners of discernment. We especially seek out excrement of exacting qualities which is often scarce in the veld where high temperatures (*that, again!*) and intense rainfall accelerate dung decomposition. No bug wants to eat rotten poop. We mostly glug in the manure of herbivores, such as dassies, animals that don't break down their food very well. So their pellets contain half-digested grass mingling in some desirably smelly liquid. It's this juice that we gulp and guzzle. But the prize-preference is omnivore ordure. These droppings are deposited by the small antelope in our district that nibble on grasses, leaves, buds, shoots, grains and nuts, but also eat insects and eggs. Savanna duikers deliver the best dung-deals!

There can be fierce competition for manure in the bundu due to not only its probable scarcity, but also the relatively short period during which the excrement is availably soft. And ball-building can be affected: the amount of food that parents roll into their brood-balls influences the size, health and emergence of their offspring. It also impacts on the reproductive success of males that have healthier beginnings and so do better at finding and fighting for mates, and of females whose sexual development relies on good nutrition.

So scuttering speedily to newly-dropped manure was crucial for me, especially at times when the veld seemed out of ordure. Amongst the rocky outcrops, where poop-piles festered few and far between: first come, first consumed. From my vantage point at the top of a dried-out cow-pat, I surveyed my surroundings... and my senses under-stimulated. Aiming my antennae ahead, feeling the future, I was sensing for a scenario when savanna manure-miracles would be less sparse, more sumptuous. When, instead of my going out to find the dung, and traipsing around for it, the dung would be all around, found. Could a dung-desiring and ravenous coprophagous creature ever shed that never-ebbing lust for more manure? And less stillness.

Chapter 8: Choosing

To fly or not to fly. That was the option. Whether 'twas nimbler in the finding to soar over these sands and outcroppings. Or to tilt tibia against a savanna of troubles and by scurrying, reach a dung-mound. To digest – to slurp, perchance to binge. I fluttered and folded my wing covers and, wishing to communicate choice to all scarabaeinae, scraped a middle-leg purposefully across my pronotum. Ay, there was the rub.

It was a small movement in a greater stillness. As he reveled in his newly-discovered and partially-deserved openness, he feelered a freedom of choice. But opportunity, rather than choice, is the gift granted freely in the veld.

Candidly, we're coprophagi. As such, our kind are really skillful at dung-discovery. It's what we do. With my specialized senses and alerted antennae, I can catch a whiff of dung from a close-by clod, or pin-point a poop-producing passer-by to stick near or to trail. Faeces further afield, I can pick up - my perceptions pull me to outlying areas where there are stacks of scoop-worthy selections. Or I can take on an aerial excrement-finding expedition, and take to, and taste, the air. The distance between dung-piles is measured in manure.

We're very strong fliers, with long flight-wings folded under hardened outer elytra. I can soar way past the dassie domains and granite boulders, in search of the perfect pat. But don't judge a batch by its cover. Not every clod has a slimy lining. In some mounds of manure, there's more to lap up than in others. It may be a dung-heap, baked and brittle and if, like a dung-beetle, its exoskeleton is hard and impermeable, it's bound to be bad. But when it's gently crusty, and wet within, it's a choice and delectable dung-pile. Finding a number-one number two is *number one!*

Like most dung-beetles, I favoured the idea of scuttling around, to taking flight. And thinking a lot of this instinct, clasping this fitting identity, I felt more at one with my species. Since emerging, I was clearly part of the coleoptera clan. Content to be a coprophage. Beautifully beetle-big, and slicker and slimier on the outside than a semi-solid duiker pellet. So, judge me by my cover.

I eat with my feet. I'm here for the manure. If it's brown, I gulp it down.

Because the modified mouth parts of dung-beetles are purposefully evolved, foreshortened limbs, these coprophagi do 'eat with their feet'. Their front legs have serrated sides to sort through dung, and are adapted for the manipulation of soft, pasty poop. The nutrients from the micro-organisms in the food need to be broken up before they are ingested; so dung-beetle mandibles, and notably their molar lobes, are shaped to finely grind and squeeze these particulates, and they have on their surfaces, bulging rows of sub-microscopic scraping tritors, which push filtered, fluid food into the preoral cavity.

Impressively imbibing insects we are! So boring braggarts we aren't. But never pooh-pooh a dung-beetle. In seasons to come, I stood pulled-together, and rose poised, when it was time to be beetle-brave, and when I showed who was the surviving fittest.

But— pointless pride… is purposeless, isn't it? Ceaselessly puffing my own pronotum was a pain in the palps. My mind was metamorphosing as I thought. My mind was metamorphosing – *as* I thought.

Nevertheless, at that moment, contemplations aside, and resurgence inside, my phenomes were feeling phenomenal. Though I was nameless, this bug was *me*. No longer a lesser larva, or puny pupae. I was tougher on the outside than dehydrated duiker-droppings. I had jaw-inspiring mandibles, and an exceptional eletrya. And under my covers lay an enviable endophallus with a compendium of chitinous sclerites. It was a time *manureal!*

Chapter 9: Growing

In the stillness of the savanna, days become evenings which become nights which become mornings, which slither into seasons. Everything under the sun metamorphoses in its time. Further out, the guiding lights of the Milky Way shine, always, constant. Across the veld there are no winter rains, so the dusts suspended over cool breezeless days throw drama at the descending sun. As the rays pass through more atmosphere the lower it sinks, sundowns become spectacular; perhaps more so, naturally, to those creatures whose vision extends over a wider spectrum than that of humans'.

The days were shortening. Dawns became deferred; and dusks, in deference, departed earlier. On the outcropping boulders, sunning lizards, eyes roving in ponder, heads quizzically flicking, lay patient in the diminishing and weakening shifts of sunshine. Dassies peeked out from their burrows to confirm the changing light and, perhaps, to admire the always glorious savanna sunset. Dung-beetles, instinctually aware of diurnal differences, scampered and rolled on, regardless. The bundu's dry chill nipped more icily as the last, loitering rays of the sun folded into darkness; and the Milky Way began glittering. Night enveloped the swaying stillness.

Insects survive in every place on the planet, except Antartica. They dislike especially cold or dry weather, and respond instinctively. However, extreme temperatures will not cause them actual physical discomfort because, unlike mammals, they have no nociceptors, so feel no pain. Contrary to often inaccurate studies, misinformed by assumption, guesswork and unnatural logic, beetles do *not* detect ambient temperatures with their antenna. And, unlike recurring human assumptions, beetle awareness *is* a product of accurate brain receptivity and processing.

'Tiny beetle-brain' *indeed!*

We feel the heat. And we know what it means to chill.

Dung-beetles possess heat-responsive neurons that alert and direct them towards more inhabitable surroundings. They can, and do, seek comfort. In pursuit of better conditions, and enhanced well-being, there are insects and animals (and humans, with their metaphysics) that relocate when the sun is in attendance elsewhere. There are shuffles when a morning mist lingers over the River Mubundovi, or when the breezes blow, taut not tender, headed nowhere. Or when the grassy clumps have turned from green to yellow to grey, and become parched monuments to past rains; or when the dung-heaps have disappeared, creatures shift. Like a rolling dung-ball, gathering momentum, life moves on. Swallows, with callings from far away, take their final swoops into retreating river waters, then soar skywards; while others must stay, and adapt. To some, this acclimatisation is a rolling dung-ball gathering mass; to others it is a brood-ball of probability. It may be a fight, or a dance. There will be discomfort, and death.

Yes, we change for our world. We don't change the world for us − because that would hurt *all* living things. That would bring damage to the veld, and spoil the savanna. That would surely slay the stillness.

In slow-motion, juddering to its own rhythms, and changing to suit only itself and inconspicuousness, a chameleon saunters across a stretch of arid ground. The rainbow-king is slow but not uncertain. Held hesitation, a withholding wait, the pause before progress, delaying before departure, are all ways, perhaps, to be sure. And, assuredly, with movement comes adaptation, and adaptation brings opportunity. Chameleons possess the ability, denied to other lizards, dung-beetles and humans, to change colour. They have an outer pigmented layer of skin covering cells which contain guanine crystals that alter the wave-length of the light reflected. This changes the hue of their skins. When the rainbow-king's mood or body temperature fluctuates, its nervous system expands or contracts specific chromatophores, and the cell colours change. Neutral tones indicate a relaxed state.

A *calmer* chameleon – maker of great change.

Excitement may induce brighter colours, like red, green or blue, while deeper shades denote stress and, especially in the throat area, indicate feelings of threat, or illness. There is a wide range in the structure of the cells covering the chameleon's body, so even adjacent patches of skin are able to reflect different colours. It is beauty-in-harmony, intelligent integration, and a lizard-lesson and blueprint for all creatures on earth. Changes in hue can be undulating, or gradual, or happen as rapidly as a dassie-in-distress finishes defaecating, or as unexpectedly as a duiker darts, after a mate's nasal-snort alarm call, and dives into the cover of denser vegetation along the riverbank.

When the time is right for it to shed its cover, and when its skin is loose, the chameleon stops eating, and turns whiter. In under a day, often in less time than it takes for the shadows of giant anthills cast across the savanna to lengthen and fade, the process is complete. The metamorphosis will have been been carefully observed by many of the creature's own all-seeing eyes. Although there is no order of importance, or any evolutionary classification, in the natural world, these rainbow-kings emit an aura of high-level omniscience; it is all-knowing, as incredible, in incomprehensibility and inexplicability, as a dung-beetle's connections to the Milky Way.

Chameleons are the most highly visually-oriented of lizards, and can see in both visible and ultraviolet light, with two eyes that move independently of each other. They each possess a negative lens, a positive cornea and monocular focusing, enabling corneal accommodation and an acute ability to judge distance. Also, the amplitude of eye movement allows the creature to see in different directions at the same time; and with pupils fused to their eyelids, chameleon eyes protrude from the sides of the head, facilitating panoramic vision.

To look ahead *while* looking around – that's advantageous!

Although they have a tendency to be highly aggressive to others of their species, chameleons are normally very shy. When alarmed or threatened, they curl into themselves tightly, darken, and play dead. But when a rainbow-king's life really ends, all the signals cease, and the creature turns deep brown, or black.

Indigenous human cultures tell of their God sending a go-go-slowly to bless men and make them immortal. The myth relates how the chameleon went on its mission, deliberately and hesitatingly, and stopped to find food along the way. A jealous, blue-headed lizard, having overheard the God's instructions, and being much quicker than the go-go-slowly, arrived earlier to tell the tribe that they would die, as all creatures did. Amid the ensuing consternation, the mortality of man was questioned, then challenged, and thereafter established. So to many men across the savanna, the go-go-slowly remains revered as a bringer of eternal life, while the agama with the blue head is a bad omen heralding death. Subsequent tribes, sometimes in peace and sometimes in war, have brought sets of beliefs from their civilizations across the many great waters. Some call the chameleon 'Jesus'.

In areas of human development, where people congregate and seek enlightenment, presumptions predominate. There are high-held hypotheses that arthropods have no emotions: it is a sad supposition, a crying shame. If humans claim they are truth-seekers, what they cannot prove, needs to be, in truth, disproven. Like poorly-rolled, dried-out dung-balls on the outcrops, poor postulations and deceit are exposed and die quickly out in the open.

As inevitable as the comings and goings of the savanna seasons, creatures that neither hibernate nor migrate face testing times in the lean, cold months of winter. The tall, brown grass thickets have turned brittle, and, to retain moisture, shrubs and trees sprout no fresh leaves. The River Mubundovi has been reduced to a blotting of bubbling, murky ponds. The bundu is bleak; there is less food, and more struggle for it. And leaner flanks and shrunken stomachs result, naturally, in diminished defaecation.

And for me – far-flung faeces-finding forays. Still scampering, but with even less spring in my scutellum, I was venturing further and further afield. My bundu-horizons were broadening, and I knew never to go too near to the wide water, on which floated too many insects who'd gone too close to the edge. As the winter deepened and the earth's crust cracked, my little flights became trips that became treks that reared thoughts of a really big journey that would end in dream-dung-land. But how was I to set off elsewhere when I was still, relatively, new out here in the outcrops? Would I become a beetle never satisfied, always driven to want wetter and weightier dung-heaps?

Dreamers and artists in the human world have suffered in passionate pursuit too. They have been damaged by desire. In wishing, they have been wounded; in craving, they have crashed. They have hoped and hurt; and some have not come back from the edge. They have cut off their ears; and they have gone mad. They have taken their own lives too.

Are homo sapiens able to conceive that other creatures – such as us coprophagi – are part of their world? Do they know that we can sense their lives? Or does their human pondering inform them otherwise? While they are still worshipping one another, or stooping to a sun, or a moon, we are in comms with the Milky Way!

But I hadn't yet encountered the human world – for *that* is another universe.

Chapter 10: Working

O h, for a muse of manure that would ascend the brightest mound of excreta. A dung-ball for a stage, feelers to react, and mandibles to munch and ingest the swell scene! Then should the working roller like himself.

Ideal food-balls, to us coprophagi, are those that swell and ooze with claggy juices. They're rolled to be moist and mucilaginous. But the days and nights in the savanna were dry and chilly, and all the good goo was gone. It was demanding, trying, to look on the succulent side. Winter dragged on and, though I'd always hated the heat, the effects of the cold – minimal manure to compress, mostly – were depressing. Only the stillness knew how the veld finds food for those hunting after they are exhausted. I positioned my palps parallel to the dung-beetle instinct that tells how toil, eating on the job, is work to be relished. Then *kungufisiza* came. Currents of questions and considerations flooded my over-analytical antenna. If you work at something you really like, it won't be toil at all: was this wisdom from any worthwhile pile? Do those who desire dung just need to eat, or are they also driven to keep rolling? Are the best dung-balls really rotated towards a better world of opportunities? *Where – if it does – does it all stop?*

Or doesn't it?

Manure was scarce, and the duikers and dassies dumped limited droppings. Opposition for ordure grew, and every day there was more scrapping for scraps. Scavenging around me, I sensed as many other dung-diggers as a beetle has spiracles. They all seemed stronger and bigger than me – I was a smaller, second-rate searcher with a less than ordinary ontogeny. And I was still a nameless nobody. It seemed that everywhere my eyes settled, other coprophagi chomped and challenged, and tackled one another as they ploughed into the dwindling dung. It was disheartening – but sensibly safe – to stand at the side, snatch at discarded scraps, and saunter off with dung-chips, dry and disregarded.

Dung-beetles are well-protected by exoskeletons. This hard but flexible outer covering, comprising of layers of interwoven proteins and chitin which are bound together into strong but flexible bundles, reduces evaporative water loss and also prevents easy, unwelcome access to vulnerable internal organs. Underneath it, there is an epidermal layer, similar to human skin, and the exoskeleton forms a sort of shell over the epidermis, in much the same way that a tortoise is unlike a dassie.

Additionally, the exoskeleton successfully repels parasites, fungi, viruses and other biological invaders, so insects can stay safe and healthy. Furthermore, pigments responsible for creating the color patterns on insects that serve to ward off potential predators are produced in the exoskeleton.

My outer covering gleamed. I was buffed and looking good – well, good enough. I shone, in humility, with a developing awareness to mind my mandibles and not show off my shell unfittingly. Afterall, the task at tarsis was: *food first!* No narcissism was needed now. Or pointless parading. Or flaunting the superfluity of self-esteem. *Kungufisza* and the reminder of rock-bottom, the specter of second-best, had returned. So, frons buried between antenna, dung-dust in my mandibles, I plodded off to under the overhang of my insignificant pupation.

There was natural protection all around me – but against what? Against the often-arduous and seldom-sweet savanna? Or against my moving forwards (or as a developing dung-beetle with new balls, backwards)? There was a gangly clumsiness in my actions. I was all-legs – so what sort of fighter, or dancer, would I ever be? Although winter kept battering my bit of the bundu, various parts of me were, at least, growing. At different times and at uncoordinated rates, tissues and organs under my now twice-shed exoskeleton, had ontogenised. Physically – and in stillness – I felt a small, poised sense of beetle-balance.

Chapter 11: Rolling

Nature abhors a vacuity. When the creatures of the savanna have supplicated for sustenance, it will come. Not as rain in this season of dryness, but here, amongst the rocky outcrops overlooking the river, in a herd of cattle being driven to cross at the Mubundovi mid-winter shallows.

The whistling, yelling humans, whisking long flank-thrashing sticks, stopped herding for a while to smoke and rest in the receding shade of a thicket of trees, and their beasts dawdled and lingered. And mooed, and grazed, and dropped dung. Their clumsy hooves, with cracked outer walls, disrespecting season-honoured savanna tracks, clunked into smaller rocks along the way, scraped carelessly along the ground, and had left newfangled dry dust-paths, spattered with ploppings.

Pats a-plenty! I sensed a sudden end to scarcity as the air was filled with the promise of a profusion of fresh poop. The long, preceding months of digging my way through hard crusty pellets, dissolved into slopping sessions of slurping and rolling. Of swigging on the job. Using my spade-shaped head to scoop out a measure of manure, my paddle-shaped antennae, and my leg-rakers to slap it spherical, one medium-sized ball was dung-done. Then another. I rolled them rapidly away to the protection of the underside of the ledge of my birth, and set them half-buried – for the time being – in the dry, soulless sand. With no time to lose, and not too many rival beetles to be bugged about, I returned to manipulating more manure.

Suddenly there, mid-pat, stood my sibling: a statuesque sight to sense. With excremental expertise and a wow-factor only the great can garner, he pushed and shoveled, he matted grasses and grit, entwined dung and dust, and formed dung-balls in moments. I studied, mesmerized by his mastery of manure. And in bogged-down observation, I learnt that balls of manure aren't merely take-away meals – they're also portable chillers. While licking his forelegs, he'd pass then through his mouthparts, spitting squelch onto them. As this fluid evaporated, it drew heat away from his legs and, in the time it takes for a swallow to swoop, or a dassie to dart down underground, he looked *cool*.

He sculpted another dung-ball, tumbled it away, and then disappeared. In the flick of a claw, and before I could splutter all over my own limbs, he was back. A second coming – my re-creator, my *Kumburukha*! In stunned reverence, I marveled at this super-scooper, this crafting coprophage, as he toiled in triumph – and I took my eye off the ball I'd slogged on and – it was gone! In my awe and elation I'd become slop-happy. I'd tossed caution to the slimy air, and before it was even a fully-rounded sphere, my sad attempt at sculpting was stolen. My ready-made package was another's tasty takenaway. Emptiness overwhelmed me, my palps flopped and flagged, and I withdrew to the fast-drying side of a centrally-plundered dung-heap.

So much dung, so little done. For how many rounds could I fight? At the least, I'd achieved something worth stealing. And I'd fashioned an idol of my super-sibling, despite his not noticing me. And I'd managed to turn things around, and rolled some dung-balls backwards. In the world of poop, where going forwards means rolling backwards, I'd mastered my ball-bearings. I'd toiled and trundled. I'd dug and dashed. I'd been on the ball, and balanced. I should've felt up in the dumps. I had proven balls! I had poop-prizes, turd-trophies, medals of manure. Yes, I *could* have my dung and eat it too!

When a beetle makes an effort, exertion makes the beetle. I look well to this day for it is on the path of life where metamorphoses lie. There is satisfaction where toil brings achievement, and beauty where there are balls. Life past is a reflection of the vision that is tomorrow. And today well-enough rolled, gives hope for seasons ahead. In the savanna, the good times that come after struggle and hardship, and after conflict and confusion, and stay in stillness, are called *Tanakai*.

No cicadas screeched cheers at his achievement. A forgotten cow farted in apathy. And in the stillness of his protective outcrop, its shelf knocked aside burying his dung-balls entirely, he had heaved himself into another day in which to roll. He had left behind the joylessness of being the consumer called 'Coprophage'. He became '*Rollo* – the Roller'.

Chapter 12: Dancing

Few sights can stretch the imagination as far as the savanna night sky. In winter, when there are seldom rainclouds to obscure the gaze, and if the moon is not beaming too brightly, the dancing arms of the Milky Way can be seen shimmering and beckoning.

A galaxy is a body of stars, gas, and dust held together by gravity. The Milky Way is the galaxy that humans say contains our solar system; and the name describes the view from earth: an arching, blurred band of lights from stars visible only as they beam together. People, who feel destined to count the stars, and create worship and wisdom from their numberings, have found in excess of 500 solar systems. New ones are being discovered all the time in the human-assumption that there may be as many as 100 billion, while it is sensed that there could be in excess of 400 billion stars out there. Down here on this planet: there are more than 10 quintillion insects.

The *Betelguese*, a star almost a thousand times larger than our sun, that gleams through the infinite blackness of the southern night skies, is positioned in the 3,500 light-years-wide Orion Arm of the Milky Way, near – well, very far, to be precise – to some of the most dazzling and enamoured of the Orion's celestial bodies. For us to count our stars would, in the strictest sense, be less enlightening than daunting. In fact, it would be impossible.

Uncountable hordes of dung-beetles converge when poop appears. Once pats are plopped, the multitudes are all in-it-to-sip-it. Excremental experience enlightens; and I'd learnt the firm way what poop-punishment it was to have one's balls grabbed. So – survival-of-the-speediest, Rollo – I was fast to learn the swift-roll quick-getaway. But, hind-sight considered, it's not easy to direct a dome of dung in a straight line, backwards. So the first skill that needs honing is how to be on top of your sphere, and get *oriented.* This means taking a mental snapshot of your surrounds, and comparing the memory of it to the current position of the stars of the Milky Way. Or when the sun is shining, a strip of polarized light perceptible only to dung- beetles of the tropics, will do. Then, it's dance-time.

Dung-beetle dance is a complex form of spinning on top of dung-balls. It is for orientation, thermoregulation and mating (somewhat similar to humans' hoppings). It is comparable to running several internal compasses in parallel, via celestial cues, and is termed 'instinctual astrology'. Timing is tantamount, and this dancing is a grasped impulse of when to proceed and when to pause.

And once the beating beetle-heart is floating in haemolymph, and antennae are on the alert: that is the dance of stillness.

I was dancing with the stars, solo in the sand. No dust-duetting. Keeping on the track, and mastering the moves. Just feeler-ing the freestyle of the veld. Forelegs good, six legs *better*. Transitions are the job of tarsi, and their dynamics do dancing. I pulled in that instinct, and kept that count. Every few levels I hit a wall but I ball-changed and full-cut, circled and climbed over it. And I danced out on top.

It's a dung life working days and nights, but always – there's shifts to do. Instinctually, but in indolence, I preferred to work, as seldom as I dared, in the early evenings or during the night. At noon, when the mid-sky sun glares, and the shades of shrubs are at their skimpiest, I'd occasionally choose to climb onto my crafted and caressed orb of ordure to give my tarsi time-out from the scorching soil. Dung is cool and every time I rose to dance, the moves were less measured. I preferred the simplicity of seldom-ness, and being laid-back. Slackness suited, and I put my hexapods up whenever I could. Roller was regularly readily relaxed.

Straight paths are easy to travel, when the lunar beams direct. But on dark and overcast nights in the savanna, it is beetle-better to be off-duty. When clouds gather, or pollution persists, dung-beetles cannot: paths become unclear, and finding direction is shaky and erratic; there is miscommunication and misunderstanding, and chaos (as with so much of human satellite messaging).

Dung-beetles got it straight! A day without dance, is a dungless day. To move-it is to step-it-up. Then when you're on top of the dung-ball, you can reach for the stars! They are always dancing. The Milky Way sways all ways in step with the savanna stillness.

Chapter 13: Sibling

First impressions last. But, in the telocopridic ecosphere, not always for long.

So it was – with the return of my super-scooping semi-sibling, my blood-brother from the same mother, who was soon to be a relative not distant enough.

Rollo's father had mated twice, at least, because he could and, possibly, instinctively, needed to. For the fittest to flourish, dung beetles loiter less and, to reproduce with rapidity, they scurry around to find other mates fairly fast. Rollo's mother had stayed boulder-side to look after her larvae, pamper her pupae, and hold vigil over her hatchings; and then she had scampered-off into the savanna, sensibly, sensing an oncoming dung-drought.

It is not for brood-balls to know, or for hatchlings to heed, or indeed, for the savanna to say, the order in which all her offspring emerged. In brood-ball cluster-etiquette, the last-rolled brood-balls, invariably poised in top positions, but with briefer manure-tenure, release first, and open the way for the lives of the less-likely. So, semi-buried, and at the edge of survival, the deep-enders or outsiders (like Rollo, or Mhezi the larva as he was known before then) would have surfaced in struggle amidst other sibling brood-balls already exposed and strewn like broken-open sarcophagi, or popped open prior to those ordained for ossification in crumbling-closed coffins.

I don't recall details, facts of the finer points of emerging, except the impression of one empty, larger and clearly-superior, brood-ball in the moistest middle of the protective overhang. My senses were hard-pressed enough adjusting to my latest limitless legroom and the aftershocks of the dazzling sunlight. The numbness at the beginning of my newest uphill battle left no time for me to check any relative dung, or close-by kin – or to be unduly alerted at the passing shade thrown by a loftier dung-beetle.

And then, spread all over me, that shadow soared. Massive mandibles. Presumptuous palps. Aggressive antennae. Big brother was eye-balling me, imperiously. Kumburukha, Prince of the Ball. Grandly, he glared. His fault-finding scathing dioptric system served, I was pushed aside. Rolled over, and sent tumbling. As I came to my senses lower down the dried dung-hill, he was there, poised over my pronotum, precariously, looming large – as I groveled, and clean forgot about the deficient dung-ball I'd almost completed. Atlas-like, he shrugged, and swaggered off, bragging of his better balls. He'd hurt my head, and scarred my scutellum with the scab that I was nothing of a roller.

'Rollo' *indeed*!

Kumburukha, the Conquering Coprophage. The telocoprid tormentor. The beetle-bully!

In none of my eyes was he any longer a Master Builder – that lowbrow, brow-beating dung-dissector. He'd hightailed off on his high-ball – with a feeble fart of mere methane and hardly a hint of hydrogen. *So* unimpressively odourless it was. But poop is thicker than flatulence. A ripened fruit does not cling to the vine. It took only one setting sun and the next rising moon for me to grasp: there were other balls to build. There were other scat-piles to scale.

Dung remained scarce, and my thirst for gooier grounds deepened. Where on earth were pastures of perfection to be found? Where are there paths paved with poop? I hankered in hungriness. My feelers flashed faith in a filthier future. Was it instinct or intuition that was the impetus to insight? Or the curse of kungufisiza goading me to go?

I'd leave the boulders and outcrops of my early metamorphosis. I'd depart from dassies and duikers. The heads of lizards would flick in futile – and fondles – farewell. A go-go-slowly would gawp, and go on. If I didn't find something new, I knew I'd find something different. What was so special in this scrap of the

47

savanna that couldn't be sacrificed, and something else sought?

I might even cross the River Mubundovi. That would be a getting-away, and a going-towards.

How could I be sure?

If the stillness spoke, I'd know.

Chapter 14: Following

It is a dry, dry world of winter. Rocky outcrops, emboldened by centuries of exposure, sit steadfast, with their boulders, seemingly unbreakable, though fissured and fracturing; they scorch in the thin midday air, and freeze in the overnight frosts. The hardiest shrubs on the savanna too, are shriveling, while seasoned trees stand sturdy. Dust-covered dassie-heads rarely appear, and when they do, it is to hardly emerge, and to squeak up to the stillness for a soaking.

Hyraxes are thought by humans to be noisy creatures, and are able to make more than 20 different sounds: they can screech and squeal and snort and chuck and yelp and whine and tweet. They create songs, typically organized and patterned into bouts, consisting of up to 30 syllables, with pauses, and lasting up to as much as several minutes each. Diva-dassie-arias are the showstoppers of the savanna!

These rock-rabbits are sociable animals, with distinct family identities, and live in colonies occasionally numbering as many as 100. Their communications are complex, and communal: rapid soundings are often emitted and heard as danger-warning signals when there is cause for alarm, and during foraging sessions there are always one or two dassies on the lookout for predators while the others nibble and browse. But when food is scarce, and foraging becomes a dangerous outing, it seems that snorts of dissatisfaction and howls of hunger echo from their burrows.

Dissatisfying it certainly was, for me to re-encounter Kumburukha, the abusive aggressor, sibling son-of-a-beetle with whom I shared a mother. Initially, I winced, wiped my palps – and peered. If any telocoprid had the strength to survive, the fitness to flourish, it was him – this commandeering coprophage, this potent tormentor. If any coleoptera had the courage to go forth, and the feelers to find food, it was this intrepid insect. And if I was sensing him, I sensed he'd be super-sensing me. But he seemed too self-sensing to be bugged by any brood-brother bother. So I tailed him, at what I considered a safe and indiscernible distance. I pursued the path of his pygidium – not close enough for discomfort, and not too far to lose trace of his tarsi-tracks. Nothing he did signaled that he'd sensed me in his shadows: arrogance is never fine-tuned. Yes, he could bury 250 times his own mass in a night. He could devour more than his own weight in a day. He could scour the surroundings in supreme super-surveillance, and build dung-balls of dramatic dimension. But ahead of me blundered a bully-beetle too conceited to be concerned about his second-rate sibling Rollo, the bug with zero to roll.

In the icy hours of the early morning, Kumburukha – the trailblazing pathfinder – took flight. I followed. I flew frantically, floundering, frequently falling out of his flightpath. But each time, phenomenally, I feeler-found it again. And I trailed tenaciously. I held heroically aloft and flapped my forewings over the vast landscape. It was a wider world than I'd ever known, and closer to the river than I'd ever been.

Boldness be my beetle-buddy!

With my head (almost) in the clouds, I climbed. I soared upwards to places and spaces where the earth matters less than its moon. I rose to where my wings were one with the wind, and where my palps were pawing the moisture droplets in the clouds. As I soared, I checked myself – knowing that beetles are less effective at generating lift than other fliers because the action of their forewings impacts negatively on their flying wings. And aware that thus, the protection afforded by the hardened forewings would come at a cost in the form of lower efficiency in flight. I recognized this short-coming, weighed-up this strange flaw in beetle-design, and... .

With concentration dizzied, and mindset misplaced, I dipped, and doubted – and lost focus on the direction of my dictator. It was momentary mistake, a fleeting faux pas. And as I plunged through perplexity, the River Mubundovi stared me in the clypeus. I veered and swooped, my vertex missing the crusted river banks by mere mandibles, and hurtled into a clod of withered grassroots. With outer-shell fully intact, but inner confidence shattered, I scrambled up and snatched for my senses. Instantly, my beetle-bearings returned, brought balance back, and I blasted off home, directed unswervingly to my hovel under the overhang.

It wasn't far – but it was the furthest I'd ever flown alone – to return to the place that never felt more like a home. After reaching new heights, with viewings over vaster vistas of veld, and so seriously sensing the scope of my landscape, I was back.

I'd found my place.

Chapter 15: Flying

Though much was taken, much was there, still; and though the savanna had sapped their strength, and all were weakened by season and fate, there remained grit in instinct, and senses to seek, to find, and not to succumb. It was a stern stillness, that spoke volumes.

With winter ending, existence in the outcrops was gravely strained. Hard-baked anthills stood as cenotaphs to lives that had gone. Dassies had died or deserted, many of their burrows stank as they became clogged corridors of sand and semi-stripped carcasses. The duikers had drifted nearer to the dangers down by the river where the vegetation was denser, and where there was no space to dart well-away from the thickets where predators lurked in small packs. No longer was every rock lizard-sentinelled. There were no flies filling the veld as the drought and dearth of droppings forced their diminishing swarms riverwards; and when the flies have flown, it is time for all to flee. Dung-beetles do not dally where there is no dung.

Rollo spent most of the day partially out of the dryness of the wintery heat, somewhat protected by the ledge that had half-buried him in a previous incarnation. Upheld between a rock and a hyrax burrow, and resting up from his upsetting encounter following and losing his brother Kumburukha, he reminisced. Dung-beetles are able to remain airborne for over 40 miles, so he knew that the River Mudundovi and the blessings beyond, were well within beetle-range, and close enough for Rollo-reaching.

Flying insects typically possess two pairs of wings. In beetles, the anterior pair has evolved into elytra, short, hardened, shell-like structures, which protect the anterior wings and vulnerable abdominal parts. So, wings and body can remain undamaged as dung-beetles are tested by, or are rummaging through, rough and unrelenting terrain. To enhance aerodynamics, the elytra are usually extended during flight, thereby significantly increasing vertical force and assisting in weight support. The wing-elytra combination generates a complex, flight-enhancing trail of air – a phenomenon not yet realized or imitated in human aviation.

I'd outgrown these rocky outcrops and was to waste no more misery around them. My thoughts were savanna-stunted, as dried-up as a dead aloe, and, it seemed most probable that I wouldn't be able to rise over the very biggest boulders, and fly freely over the veld. But there was a world elsewhere! As low as I seemed then, the higher I sensed I'd fly. Bugs are given four wings to rise above the earth, and surge over what grows in and on and above it. Dung-beetles were designed to surface and soar over their own brood-balls, to glide over trees and tracks, and above fences and fire-guards, and float far from the flux of rivers.

Mubundovi, my back-side!

As that day died, and the blackness of night staggered across the savanna, I emerged from under my ledge. Antennae-tuned and elsewhere-oriented, with hind-wings unfolded and inflated, tibia-tightened and femur-forward, I took off. I arose from, and left behind, the bundu of my birthplace.

A slight breeze played across the veld, and sky-mists condensing into cloudlets, swirled lightly above. I zigged over the empty dassie burrows, and zagged above a lone duiker and her lamb. The Milky Way glowed and glistened, and leaned in to give direction to my search for the trace of the track of that treacherous semi-sibling I'd failed to follow before.

If you fly high enough, perspectives realign. As the rocky outcrops pebbled out of perception, I could see the other side of the river, coppices hugging winding roads, and the farmlands furtive beyond. I crossed the stillness – which was *nothing* like the buzz I was in – below, and as I accelerated, scared dung-less, but determined, I caught a whiff, then a blast, of distant droppings. New smells don't come to coprophagi who sit, but *do* to those who soar. If ever there was a higher point since

55

pupaeing, and a turning point in my metamorphosis, it was *then*. Boldness became a friend! There are more things in heaven and earth, Rollo, than were dreamt of in your second-rate brood-ball of poop. I saw the lights. Fluttering full-throttle, and closing in on the scent secreting buoyancy and inspiring assurance, I presented my palps, and descended – and touched the face of Dung.

To hiss goodbye to winter, the first of the summer showers flecked the farm. The damages of the drought would be curbed and cleansed, and the riverbanks unclogged. Mud-holes and murky pools were splattered to streaming. The dance of reliving had begun to whirl, as the soul of the savanna was shaken into showers, and the earth surged in stillness.

Chapter 16: Feasting

Some seasons ago – never mind how long precisely – having little or no poop in my palps, and nothing in particular to munch in my mandibles, I knew it was a good idea to fly around a little and see the watery parts of the farm. I'd bypassed the river, but crossed the ashy black line of a fire-guard that the farmer had burned days ago… and which led down a road to the places inhabited by humans.

Homo sapiens are ubiquitous – the term means 'wise man', and may need to be explained. They are terrestrial primates, one of several species grouped into the self-created and personally-named genus '*Homo*', and the only ones not yet extinct. They are easily distinguished by their usually erect posture, and as they are not covered by a protective outer exoskeleton, are extremely vulnerable. External skin pigmentation may vary from off-white to deep-brown, and they are typically covered in patches of flexible setae, which they call 'hair', sometimes unnatural and of varying pigmentations, that is insensitive to touch, taste, sound, smell or light. For mobility, and to compensate for the limited efficiency of only two remaining legs, they have developed external, often distantly-detached and frequently sizeable modes of terrestrial, land, sea and aerial transport which facilitate complex systems of territorial maneuvering. Their forelegs have developed into tarsi ending in five dexterous, independently-movable extensions, tipped with barely-functioning and sometimes multi-coloured claws. They have poorly-developed, ineptly immovable mandibles; two simple eyes, sometimes with additional lenses attached, and relatively narrow vision. Humans use symbolic communication systems to interact, creating complex and chaotic social groups, in a society held, often loosely, together by a variety of rituals, social norms and values, and an instinctual need to judge and measure everything. They are unable to communicate effectively with any other living organisms. They can exhibit curiosity and sensitivity, and have social awareness, but are prone to excessive aggression and kill each other indiscriminately. *Homo sapiens* exist in all regions of the planet, adapting semi-effectively by taking on the outer coverings of other once-living organisms. They are territorial, and prefer to live and operate mostly indoors in self-constructed, highly variable dwelling spaces. They are omnivorous, often gluttonously, though recent evolutionary moves are towards being more herbivorous and exercising dietary restraint. And humans don't generally feed on the excrement of others: they call it 'shit'.

On Dunghill Farm where humans lived and toiled, the laws of nature had been upended, and the lives of many creatures were controlled by a few. There were times where nights could be turned day-like at the flick of a switch, and places where movement across the land was deliberate and loud – and damaging, where the stillness was shattered by motors and machines.

But where there's poop, there's prosperity, and there were piles of poop aplenty, mountains of manure. Spoilt for choice, insects indulged interminably. And I found myself searching through such a sumptuous selection!

Despite desiring only ordure, dung-beetles are diners of discernment. They are most attracted to omnivore dung since it is nutritionally superior, and it exudes the right amount of odour to make it easy to find. These dung-dining crawlers value variety in their diets and, to avoid manureal monotony, may shuffle past any same-ol'-same-ol' soilings, to leave spoor in manure, seeking more exotic excrement, and moister, muckier prospects.

I'd found a *farm*! I fleeted furiously from pat to pile, sampling stacks of varieties of mounds of manures never before fancied. Every night was a delight, every day an indulgence. Incredible, intense ingestings. Frenetic, frenzied feastings in palaces of poop. Bigger than any bundu buffet, or savanna smorgasbord! There were dunes of droppings from hay-eating horses and cud-chewing cattle. There were loads of load-offs from shed-sharing sheep and trough-tippling pigs. The poultry-poop – was less worth pursuing. The chickens were cooped-up in an overcrowded fowl-run, fed on cornmeal pellets and human scraps, and their imbalanced intake produced paltry plops of poop that smelt too much like... well, *shit*.

What one eats, one excretes: as all the farm animals consumed mostly pellets or crumbles, all human-made, from similar cornmeal compounds of cereal or lugume-amalgams, amongst the coprophagi there was a preponderant sense of gustatory monotony. There was a deranged dog too, permanently panting, and yapping and yelping, chasing cows and hounding horses, and dispersing doo-doos too indiscriminately and distantly to deem worthy of wandering waywardly towards. And there were humans, whose droppings were deemed the deposits most desired at Dunghill Farm.

But the preferred people-poop proved inaccessible to insects. It sloshed away down subterranean passages feeding vast cement-lined, brood-ball-like cavernous cisterns - from which I turned, in trepidation. I knew too well that my days of consumption in dark underground mausoleums of manure were *not* to be revisited.

The farmyard of faeces fed *many* more faces than the outcrops could ever have sustained. Throngs of flies flew everywhere, and settled to suck where their maggots munched, and where worms wiggled, and larvae lay in swallowing lavishness. Hordes of marauding coprophagi labored relentlessly at and in the embankments of available ordure. The manure-scape moved and shimmered as insects prodded and poked and scurried and scuttled and scampered – and scuffled.

There were countless other dung-beetles too. I watched in alarm, anxiously confirming that where there's manure, there's competition – and marauders! Bands of beetle-thieves tackled and tumbled and raided. Casting caution to the aromas, they didn't work from the inside of a pat or from the centre of a pile to be protected from any outside predators, as they would've had to in the veld. These dungies, running warm, scuttering across the scat, could level a pile of freshly-shunted bovine poop well before the cows came home. And every so often, that lone-ranging hound lumbered by – sniffing and snapping, licking a lot, gnawing a little – and eating nothing.

The insect world is an ecosphere of cooperation. Dung-beetles may not collect in communal nests or hives, but they do connect. After abandoning his bundu outcrop, and being abandoned by his sibling, Kumburukah, Rollo sensed strongly that having contact with others of his kind could be crucial.

As opening-communication signals, I tried trickling some chemical releases, but there was no comeback from the crowds. The slogging swarms remained absorbed and interested in their own ingestings, massively inattentive to my endeavours. A nearby dung-beetle duo stayed slopping and sculpting, scanned my scutellum, then bugged-off, bowling their brood-balls back to protective and greener pasturelands. So I tried pulling some poses. I made a few moves, followed by a series of unsure scrapes. Then shifted to more indelicate scratches. And greater grindings, and gaudier gratings. Still no response.

Was it because there was no stillness? I stood silent. The laws of the savanna, it seemed, held no sway in stables and stalls and sties. But there *was* deliberation and depth in dung, and I wasn't about to lose my appetite over the inattention of others. I was plonk in the middle of a period of plenty, safe in stacks and swells, an ecstatic coprophage in heaps of happiness. I was *digging* all that dung!

New energies fuelled new expeditions in excrement. It wasn't enough to merely scoff – I needed to wallow in all the watery wonders. I was learning a significant lesson: with humans came excessive excrement. Smells were summons-signalling that *now* was the time, that *this* was the place. There were no seasons of ebb and flow on the farm, no times of little and then less. No reasons for rolling right then, and no saving slop for tomorrow. So what was I – a dweller and not a roller now? In my haste for taste, my greed for need, in my dancings in dung, I'd left the savanna. I'd surpassed its stillness.

Chapter 17: Human Being

It is growing quieter and rapidly darker on the farm. I am sitting in the evening shadows, on an out-cropping ledge of concrete that may once have been part of a wall that kept farm animals contained, and safe. I watch in fascination as hundreds, literally, of dung-beetles are working their ways through the surrounding piles of horse manure. In the Coleoptera insect order, Onthrophagus genus, dung-beetles are classified into the superfamily Scarabaeoidea, subfamily Scarabaeinae, family Scarabaeidae, scarab beetles, of which there are more than 5000 species. A large number of those I can see right now, are precisely what I am here to observe: *Scarabaeus satyrus*, the nocturnal African dung-beetle. I plan to complete my research in the next six to eight weeks, which should be enough time to decide on the most interesting aspects of satyrus life for my final thesis and lecture focus.

It was dusk almost an hour ago. The shadows of the sheds and stables had lengthened and then disappeared. I had taken a stroll. I wanted to quell the excitement and anticipation I was feeling at having arrived at Dunghill Farm earlier this afternoon. Then, perhaps, nearer midnight when the time came, I would fall asleep more readily. But I knew that the novelty of unfamiliar surroundings and newly-acquainted people would keep me up until late. The stars were out, and with the stench of manure heavy in the air, my giddy thoughts drifted back to the events of the last few hours.

It was hot in the late afternoon when I turned off the tarred highway at the designated cluster of home-made signposts. I lowered the volume of my booming travel music and drove, continuing more carefully and quietly, along the grassy crowns of the farm roads. And when confronted by an oncoming tractor, we both had to slow right down and veer off the two central ruts in the road, into the gravel ditches. Then, with a friendly wave, I wheelied back onto the dirt tracks, and drove on in dusty and bumpy determination. It was manageable fun. I passed through the shades of spreading mufuti and msasa trees. There were barbed-wire fences and I had to stop the car to get out and open – and carefully close – a wonky steel and wire-bound gate. Driving over the black strip of fireguard, a burned belt of land cleared of all inflammable vegetation so as to halt any spread of uncontrolled veld fires, I crossed the farm boundary. I entered the space of my new home.

The farmhouse was a white-washed brick building, modest and with a pretty garden. A dog barked madly, and non-stop. Mr and Mrs Hidebound, flanked by two children, stood out on the front lawn to greet me. The couple were effusively welcoming, while the young adolescents said politely little.

'It is a great honour to have someone from a university staying at our place, Miss,' the farmer declared. 'Please call me Bertie, and this is Johanna, and the kids are Sonny and Sissie.' He pointed, clarifying exactly who was who.

'I'm Kuwiwirana, happy to be here.'

I was shown across the veranda and into their sprawling sitting-room. Cats were scooped off the couches and lumbered off across the flecked, polished-cement floor, and I sat down hugged in soft, clumpy furnishings. A white-haired old woman sat in a shallow armchair bent over herself in a far corner, in silence. The dog stopped barking.

'*What* is your name?' Sonny asked deliberately.

'Please call me *Rana* – or *Wiwi* if you like.'

The adults seemed satisfied with 'Rana' and nodded in agreement, while the children snickered and fidgeted.

'*Wiwi*'s a silly name,' the boy denounced, and was quick to receive a smart papa-cuff across the head. As tears welled-up in his eyes, he skulked away, mobile phone in hand and younger sibling in tow.

High tea at Dunghill Farm was served. Teapots were kept hot and decorated with bright tea cozies. And the ritual of dunking rusks was observed. It gave us all something to busy ourselves with, while I was describing my interest in dung-beetles. Mr Hidebound was quick to offer what he called 'a tour of my estate', and to let me know that I also had his permission to take a tour of his wife's garden 'in due course'. He had a very Englishman kind of bravado, and did most of the talking. I was not yet comfortable enough to call him 'Bertie' and he seemed confused about how to address a younger woman like me – a *university* person. Had he realized then that I was of mixed ancestry, he may well have been even less at ease. Johanna, on the other hand, appeared composed and cordial. She was somewhat matronly in her obvious friendliness, and adamant that I would 'love' her garden. I was not introduced to the old woman. Then, my suitcase and I were taken to the 'spare-room', and I washed up.

'This is the shed for the gardening tools, and that building with the corrugated iron roof is my workshop – you don't want to be in there when it's raining hard,' he chuckled. 'Come here and see the stables – I have seven horses, and over there are the pigsties, and that's the sheep-shed. If you can't see it, you can smell it.' Before I'd had the chance to unpack anything, or thank Johanna for the small posy left on my pillow, I was on a tour of the outhouses, and beyond. 'Every few months, I fill these pens with calves and turn them into fattened heifers and steers, and send them off to the slaughter. I make beef here." He chortled, and turned to me – and stared, momentarily. I was unsure of what reaction he needed, so meekly smiled. Mr Bertram was clearly proud of what he had achieved in two decades as a farmer, and justifiably so. The farmyard was a smooth (and slightly smelly) operation.

A dog came bounding up to us, pawed the ground in front of me, and barked – some more. Sonny followed, then Sissie. It soon became clear that sending Sonny was an established way to tell the farmer that he was needed elsewhere. So off he trundled, faithful dog yapping at his side. As he turned past the shed wall, his son was quick to speak.

'*Wiwi* isn't a name.' It was almost an accusation. 'So are you gonna live with us?'

'I'd like it if you called me *Rana*. And I'll call you *Mwana* – it will be our little secret.' I explained that this was what my parents had called me when I was a child, and that I'd liked it, and that when he grew into a man like his father, I would call him *Murume*.

'I have enough names I don't need already: Gabriel, Andries, William, Daniel... !' He was looking up from his mobile phone.

'Those are good names.' I was trying to lighten his antagonism, and so I took out my phone, smiled, and showed him how to look up what they meant. 'See here: "Gabriel" means "Strength from God", and "Daniel" means "God is my judge".' I was scrolling frantically looking for reassurances. '"William" means that you have a strong heart, and "Andries" means that you are manly.'

'And he's *not* my father,' Sonny snapped back. 'My real dad was taken away by another lady and we don't know where he is.'

I was out of my depth. And surrounded by coprophagi, I lifted one up.

'Do you know what this is?' I probed lamely. Sissie winced and, repulsed at my handling a dirty dung-beetle, strode off, murmuring something about 'washing… hands'.

Of course young Mwana knew what the dung-beetle was. The boy had grown up around animals and insects. After glaring in my direction, he edged towards me, and tilted his head. I froze. Then suddenly, he grabbed the creature from my hand and hurled it against the wall. He stomped on it, repeatedly, and crouched over the shards.

The night is dark, and only a crudely hung light bulb, dangling against the nearby stable wall, throws some glow over the dozens of beetles all actively digging and rolling. Well, almost all of them. One lone youngster is looking on, seemingly in some kind of contemplation. It rolls a little, then stops, antennae flicking, and rolls again – how unusual – reminding me that I have a fresh and strange bed to go to. I walk towards the white-washed house, and feel a strange wind, almost a sense of stillness, blowing across the farm.

Once I fell asleep, I slept soundly, and in the morning I woke to life on the farm, and a bedside small mug of tea. Sunlight streamed into my room. Although the fowl-run was more than 100 metres away, past a grove of mango trees and at the other end of the vegetable garden, I could hear a pair of crowing roosters. Sissie knocked gently on the door.

'Breakfast is ready. We eat because it's eight o'clock.'

It is a real farmer's breakfast, generous and heavy. I am shown to the guest seat at the end of the table, from where Johanna ordinarily operates. She is a watchful hostess – the efficient farmer's wife. Bertram presides at the head of the table, and stays long enough to eat everything served, and to have a break from his early morning rounds on the farm. He follows a morning ritual: pushing his chair away from the table, exhaling deeply, wheezing, taking up his cup of coffee, and lighting another cigarette. The children are obedient eaters, quick to excuse themselves once the cigarette smoke sends them outside 'to play'. The silent old woman has not joined us.

With apron tied and secateurs neatly pocketed, Johanna is showing me around her flower garden. It is brick-lined and pretty. I have been lent a large-brimmed, straw sun hat to replace the useless baseball cap I had brought. And, coated with a smear of sun-block and some squirts of insect-repellant I knew I would need, I feel ready for any farm garden circuit.

'I grow what I think is nice,' she beams, squirting hosepipe in one hand and insecticide spray-bottle in the other. 'I don't mind if the foreign flowers are together with the indigenous. It makes an interesting mix. See, this red hot poker is quite happy right here by the chrysanths. The flame lily is fine next to the death lily. But, Rana – and please call me 'Jo' – you must always have the tall ones at the back and the small ones in the front.' She instinctively squirts at a clump of forget-me-nots. 'And the pests - they prefer the foreign plants too.'

Sonny joins us, and Sissie is dawdling in a distant flower bed, prodding at her phone. Johanna sees a snail and no sooner has she flicked it onto the path than Sonny steps on it, crushing it slightly.

I bite my tongue.

'Oh,' Johanna is surprised at seeing a dung-beetle, 'so big. These critters get here with the manure we bring from the sheep-kraal to fertilise the garden.'

'Kill! Kill!'

'No, Mwana – er, Sonny! These are good insects,' I cut in, gently – I hope. I feel some defence is necessary. But he has had his fun spoilt and is disappointed, and I feel a need to explain. As I begin, Sissie joins us. I am relying on facts to give me some needed authority and credibility.

'They do not bite. And they are not pests. In fact, they kill bacteria when they eat and when they bury the manure. They help farmers... ' and realizing that that was not headed in an empathetic direction, continue: 'They carry dung away from places where there may be too many actual pests that are multiplying. *Dangerous* parasites. So the habitats of those bad, bad pests are removed...' – too condescending now – 'therefore their numbers are greatly reduced. A healthy population of dung-beetles can decrease the numbers of internal parasites excreted by grazers...' I was becoming a mind-numbing lecturer, and my listeners were losing interest.

'Bertram tells me that the papers from your university say you are doing a License of Veterinary Examination – L-O-V-E – project on dung-beetles.' She sniggers at her recognition of the apparent irony, then titters openly, and waves her heavily freckled arms about. She is giving the flower beds a good soaking.

Sonny is still looking on. It is more of a blank than disbelieving frown, and I feel better that he seems to have restrained his hostility. Then, seemingly as a challenge to my higher learning, and as evidence that he too has powers of observation and deduction, asks, 'Do only girls get freckles?'

His hand rests on his mother's wrist mottled with overlapping freckles, as he gazes up into my brown-speckled face.

'Ok, then,' Johanna smiles, 'be a good boy and take the dung-beetle to the stables. Maybe it's lonely. Maybe it wants to be with all its friends.'

Chapter 18: Befriending

A ll insects are equal but some are more equal than others. Where animals are farmed, when there are hordes of marauders, some roll more unequally than most.

While I celebrated being in new spaces in the landings of plenty, my developmental disadvantages were still the enemy within. I frequently felt inferior. The shadow of Kumburukah had scarcely shortened – some fears, I fear, never fade. Once scarred, always scared. Larger, more self-possessed dung-beetles were still able to grab my balls, and smaller beetles seemed slyer and swifter, keener to roll faster and readier to restart more furiously. Roll up your trocanters, *Rollo*! I prompted myself – who else was there to remind or to be reminded? Having metamorphosed a triflingly few times, I knew that it wasn't only ageing creatures that talk to themselves. It was a far, far better thing to be mired in mediocrity in a palace of poop, than be second-best in a bundu of barrenness. I'd survived in a savanna of scarceness, and I'd lifted myself out of dried dung-heaps before. I'd been down in the palps, and I'd risen. Ascending is an abdominal achievement, revival is all in the vertex. Pep-talk-prepared, pronotum up, frons forward and mandibles down – I was open for any opportunity in ordure, ready to delve into any dung-dispute. I was an insect set to suck and seek strength – and succeed.

No sooner had I plucked up the beetle-bravado to proceed, than above me loomed a labrum of largeness. Mammoth maxillae more immense than I could remember – maybe mightier than before. Had my fear mutated into mindlessness? Time-transfigured, does dread develop and destroy? I retracted in fear. Was it...? The mandibles were too monumental, and just too great to be true – as it transpired.

I'd found Stag, my substitute-sibling. A beetle-brother, a Colophon kinsman, a Scarabaeidae counterpart – an insect in a different class indeed. He became the partner who balanced me, the creature who comforted me, and the teacher who turned me into a truthfully confident coprophage. He knew his poop, and took dung from *anyone*. I knew him as 'Stag' always, a stag in all ways. There was everything in that name – never a need for change. We scraped and clicked immediately. In no time we were mutually muckraking – marvellously. Complementary coprophagi, we complimented each other in manureal moisture, flattering in flatulence and, without my recognizing its foundation, my erudition in excrement had begun.

Stag showed me that dung-beetles are the earth's most powerful insects. I learnt that we're the strongest creatures on the planet in relation to our body weight. Even in my earlier days, I'd sensed the stirrings of strength as I pulled poop more than a thousand times my own body mass (that's equivalent to an average human hauling five lorry-loads full of other humans). And, being males, we had extra exceptional strength, not just for pushing dung-balls but also for fending off male competitors in mating manoeuvres. This gentle giant completed me with a coprophagous-confidence that took me to places, across piles and into pats, that are only pipe dreams in poop.

'You gotta dance in the dung, dude. First: decide if you're more of a dweller or a roller or a tunneller, ok? Then: you hone in. It's all about focus. The easiest and most laid-back moves are for dwellers. They're basic, bro. You squat, abdomen in the dung, and feed. And up – and feed again. Rudimentary, Rollo.' Despite his huge ungainliness, he demonstrated clearly, and directions were upfront and easy to follow. 'There's no weight resistance, and there's no need for isolation. You'll be sitting surrounded by maggots and worms and fly larvae. And you do zilch but dwell, and digest. Got it?'

It was a more than a mouthful, a weighty carry-on. Simply 'sitting' suited me, though. No need for exertion – I was enticed by the effortlessness. Instinctively, however, it felt *wrong*. To air my dissent, I thought a cleansing chemical exchange, a discussion to diss his directives, would be in order... but there was no time to argue.

'Ok, so try this, then. You call yourself Rollo,' he set up the challenge, 'so it'll come naturally to you. You gotta do the groundwork first, rollout a few rudimentary reps, and then shovel along. You'll feel some weight resistance, but try not to rest. Don't take a timeout. Roll, over – and repeat. Keep patting, and turn, turn, and turn. Get in plenty of reps. *Plenty of reps.*'

I was around familiar faeces, but found the exercise strenuous, and the 'rudimentary' reps tiresome and – well, *repetitive*. With little effort, barely deploying his palps, my mammoth mentor had sculpted his sphere, a ball bigger than me, while I was still fumbling formlessly in the dung.

'Ok, that's enough for tonight. Well grasped and pushed, Rollo. This, bro, is for you.' He'd offered me his prize dung-ball. Some bugs are born great, some achieve greatness, and others have greatness thrust on them.

I clambered up onto Stag's sensational sphere of dung – and danced around. We looked at each other, from dung-beetle to stag-beetle, and from stag-beetle to dung-beetle, and from dung-beetle to stag-beetle again; and in the stillness it was nearly impossible – in my mind, at least – to say which was which.

Chapter 19: Flailing

Night was the time for nocturnal coprophagi to rummage and roll. The stables were saturated with the sweet smells of horse manure, and the sties simmered in the pongs of pig poop, and when the feed pens were full of calves for fattening, there blew across the gardens of Dunghill Farm, the heavy tang of fresh, young cattle manure. Horses disperse their dung with indifference, heads held nonchalantly high, while pigs pick a place and stick to it. Cattle wave and lift their tails indiscriminately, and plop pats anyplace, and if their back legs aren't positioned away from the faeces-freefall, they too can take a smearing.

Excess doesn't diminish desire, and cravings aren't curbed by abundance. Does poop aplenty provoke forward-looking, backward-rolling, beetles to a wariness that soon there may be leaner times? Even where there was excessive excrement, wars over dung-ball building waged on. Where the density of competing males brought the bigger beetles to battle more readily, I sensed my insignificance. Staying out of fights seemed sensible. But *any* rolling I did was likely to attract dirty double agents. I'd started shaping my first ball of the night, slapping, sculpting – and considering. Is it not possible to create a realm where everybody has an equal, or at least a reasonable, chance of peace and prosperity? Are we so consumed in the relentless pursuit of poop that... .

Femur-flick! Spur-swish! My dung-ball was thrust aside. Instinctively, my feelers froze – and I clawed out. I caught the strawy edge, and yanked. It twirled and slumped. As the raider rallied, and snatched and shoved, we tussled and wrangled. I was all legs, flailing and flapping femurs, and a tarsis here and a tibia there. Clypeus clash, frons confrontation and – *flip!* I, Rollo, was sent *rolling* in the dust, and landed, pygidium-up, sternites exposed and showing more metasternum than was right. I was an insect inverted. Flip-flopped. Overturned. A belittled bug, once again beaten.

Mutadzi! Thug! The brute-of-a-beetle turned tail, sprang sideways, and scuttled off with my scruffy semi-sculpture. *Mbhava! Thief!* – and left me done and dusted, and devoid of dung. Recoiling in shock and disgust and anger and revenge, and with flashes of Kumburukah and silhouettes of Stag towering over, and shockwaves of what should've been and... .

A female had filched my effort, not merely my excrement. My first confrontation with a lady-bug – daunting indeed, and she was big, bad and bullying.

Once more, *kungufisiza* – I knew it – had scrambled my senses. With every eye I possessed, my focus had been foiled – yet again! How could it have happened? The questionings continued to cascade. Without this exoskeleton, how much haemolymph would I've lost? Can any-bug hurt you without your permission? Were females to be forever fierce and foreign – and unfathomable? When would I know my enemy?

Hell is other poop-pushers.

Chapter 20: Developing

I trundled from the stables, and with only the Milky Way as friendly guide, my fate hung in the stars, my destination: elsewhere. I considered the rocky outcrops, and craved dassie droppings and duiker dung, a lizard's overlook, or merely a moment of savanna stillness. I was down in the dumps in the Dunghill darkness, skulking in the stable excrement, prodding pitiably through piles of palp-worthy poop. Then, from the far side of the sheep-kraal, I sensed a familiar chemical connection, a femur friendliness of recognizable leg-rubbings, and the stirring sounds of mandibles scraping, sweetly. I spotted Stag, 'hangin' with the boys'.

'Hey, I know you're not a tunneller, Rollo. You'd never bury your balls when you could shift them. You *roll* them places, far away from the full-on action round a fresh plopping. You don't need that kind of resistance, bro. Those negative phases are fundamentally not for you. And that's not your sticking point at all. 'Cause you don't wanna damage that sparkling shell, that cool cover of yours. You're a roller, *and* a shaper and a mover,' he beamed.

Some stags are such sweet-talkers. And it was almost as though we were back together, the two of us, an unlikely pair, with me dancing on high. But the delight – as it so often is – was short-lived. When he told me he'd stood aside as he spotted my earlier struggle, the flattery faded. Didn't Stag know then that I'd needed support? Where were his beetle-instincts? My beetle-*bro*? What happened to the bug-blood-connection? I felt the distance. And the difference. The 'fundamental' dung-detachment. He was a mere bystander, pushy and weighty, and solid, while I was a less-than-frenetic freestyle spinner of transitions and dance dynamics, and ball-changes and full-cuts and circles. He was simply a stag-beetle that had only been through three instars, he'd never even been a larva – he was no roller. We're both coprophagi, certainly – but he is no Rollo.

'It's a fundamental defeat, that's part of dung-beetle development, bro. You lost a scuffle, you're a dung-duel down. It's the end of nothing. If it doesn't bug you tomorrow, then who cares now?' I tasted sense in his logic, and sensed compassion in his concern. And, not so alone in that world so distant from the outcrops, I rested quietly, without overthinking – *kungufisiza* in check. I knew that if I just dwelled in Stag's simple optimism, and fundamental farm fathomings, I'd roll through. I'd be riding high. 'You can't be the best every time, man, so be at your best at the right time.' I couldn't disagree. 'Look at yourself: multiple-jointed plates. You've got muscles attached to an exoskeleton that really moves! You can shift anything, bro.'

Both my regard for Stag, and my confidence in his capacity to make me into a fearless fighter, were ignited, and then prospered. In the nights that followed, he taught me the stag-beetle basics of kicking, hitting, wrestling and grabbing. I trained in movement and in stillness, for strength and speed, and for flexibility and endurance. And I learnt the need for balance. I slap-kicked and dropped-down and arm-stretched and arm-wheeled. He took me through a plethora of paces, fundamentally at first, then building to speed. I could do the combination – rooster stance, toe pointed down, forward step and inside crescent. With chicken claws and horse-hoof punches. My front limbs were weapons wielded in unarmed combat. During a battle, the main objective – I'd grasped it! – is to dislodge opponents' tarsal claws with my mandibles, thus disrupting their balance, then heave my rivals off the path and proceed in pursuit of better balls. Or, as I was to discover later, a worthier lady-bug. After all, my flagellum was, fundamentally, proportionately, far bigger than my mentor's. 'Never fight to kill, bro – only to overturn. To let the loser scuttle away, is the true sign of victory.'

From semi-submerged second-rate bundu beginnings, I'd transformed into a battle-ready beetle, all set to dance on the dung-ball of my desire. Lord over the flies and their larvae, and the maggots and worms, and all the other beetles! I was massively appreciative of Stag's instruction, mightily motivated by my metamorphoses, and remained in awe of his awesome stag-ness. He'd liberated my head and my thorax and my abdomen. And I knew that a ripened sour-plum doesn't cling to the shrub: my bundu background could never leave me. The beetle can leave the savanna but the savanna never leaves the beetle. In exhilaration and with new senses of independence, I wished him a warm smear-well and left him 'hangin'', near the tool shed, 'with the boys', to be in with the outsiders, to find his own kind.

Stag was unrealistic enough to be an aspiration, yet within the realms of realism to not be a disillusion. He was my mentor in manure, an idol in excrement. He showed me that in the heat, the ball is cooler than the earth. In my nights with him, I'd learnt how to mash manure, pulp poop to paste, smear in style, and crush with confidence, to find and have the balls. And to dance – in and around and through and with and *on top of dung*.

Chapter 21: Human Rating

Arm elbow-deep up a cow's anus, he is reaching for dung. He scrapes around inside with his fingers, cups his hand, and scoops out as much manure as he can.

'Slowly in, around, then gently out. And repeat. Until the passage is clear,' Dr Navors, the veterinarian is showing Mr Hidebound the farmer how to clean a cow's lower intestine prior to artificial insemination. It is a messy process, and splodgy but not dirty. Dr Navors seems also to be enjoying the attention he is commanding.

I am standing with Farmer Bertram near his feed pens, justifying my board and lodging by telling him much of what I know about dung, and the creatures that depend on it. We have just finished eating breakfast.

'Cattle manure is often the wettest, and is most full of gastric juices. It is anywhere between 70 to 90 percent moisture,' I continue. 'A cow's digestive system extracts only 10 to 30 percent of the nourishment its food contains, and shunt out the rest as dung.' His bushy eyebrows arch when he hears 'shunt'. 'That is why farm feed often contains large amounts of more easily digestible nutrients.'

'Yes, don't want the cattle in the pens to be...' his left eyebrow bristles as he pauses, searching momentarily for the word, 'poeping' out all that expensive feed. Instead of carrying it on their bodies – putting on weight, more beef, you know.'

I nod. Then the vet calls the farmer over to learn how the semen is sucked into the long pipette tube which is then inserted into the cow being inseminated. I do not feel invited, and turn to observe the busy dung-beetles around me. I hardly think Bertram really wants to hear about why dung-beetles produce a greater number of balls with horse faeces than with cattle manure. He might give me a price analysis of how much more expensive it is to feed horses than cattle. I confess that I tend to go into long-winded lecture mode when talking about my areas of study and assumed expertise. I suppose dung can get boring – to others. And I chortle thinking I could let Bertie know that dung-beetles actually prefer omnivore droppings so they would be headed for his excrement first!

I had met Dr Futiel 'Footie' Navors before. He was an external examiner observing me on a previous Scientific Hospitals Intern Training Project. He is extremely well-educated and certified, and incredibly impolite. His academic standing and practical expertise are as well-respected as his social dalliances are not. He is a noted veterinarian, an agronomist and a boor. As I pursue higher qualifications, I hope I will not achieve his level of infamy. He is also Johanna's brother.

The dung-beetles interest me more than the people. They sense the glistening cow manure as it emerges. It must smell so good to them! Almost as soon as it is splashed onto the surrounds, hundreds of flies and beetles will arrive, followed by other insect predators, feeding on the coprophagi. By tomorrow morning, a drying crust will have formed over the surface of the manure pat, slowing further evaporation. It will take over a month before the dung becomes odourless, more fibrous and crumbly. Many organisms will have benefited from the manure, much of which is gradually carted away and buried by dung-beetles.

A recent scientific study found that a cowpat could hold over 1000 developing insects. Multiply that by up to ten pats produced by each cow per day and you get more than two million insects (mostly flies) per year feeding on the manure of a single cow. The statistics are astounding, and here I am, watching this incredible world in action.

It is nightfall and I have returned to continue my observations. I want to see as much as I can learn. Dung-beetles are eating nonstop. Many are also creating dung-balls and some occasionally are fighting over them. The tussles are swift and the loser is tossed aside but remains alive and well enough to begin working fairly immediately on the next dung-ball. There are noteworthy moments when one of them completes a ball, is poised on top to orientate itself – or perhaps is it to celebrate and show-off – and then scurries it away for safekeeping. Other battles between beetles are more intense when the fight is for a mate.

Three male dung-beetles at the side wall of the tool shed draw my attention. I lean in to observe. They appear to be mating with each other in turns. I know that in the animal kingdom this action of same-sex creatures going through the motions of courting is nothing extraordinary. In fact, it is often considered necessary. Some observers believe that male insects that mate with other males are simply making a mistake, or they may not recognize females because their social conditioning has been different. More extensive studies claim that same-sex activity helps males to have more offspring by reducing mating competition. Other males may be distracted or even injured, so social alliances or dominance over them is established. Similar outcomes may apply to female couplings. Also, more courtship practice could improve heterosexual performance for both genders. I reflect on observations that humans could do well to understand that nothing that is natural is abnormal.

Chapter 22: Passing

Normal families are all alike; every abnormal family is unbalanced in its own ways. There are parents who are separated from each other, and their offspring. There are siblings who stay together when they could be better balanced alone; brothers who battle brothers, and sisters who forsake sisters. There are unlikely connections that continue, and tender ties that are torn apart. But there are always correlations that connect all creatures. And all the while, there are outsiders who exist on the edge so that others can stay centred.

Also, there is Benzi, a barking beast. In the savanna '*benzi*' means 'stupid', though it is not well known or widely needed because it is never used to describe what is natural in that world. But in places where humans exist, and keep 'pets', it can be apt and appropriately applied; and here on Dunghill Farm it *is* the dog. In the same way as a dung-beetle and a stag-beetle may be unlikely partners around a cow pat, pooches and people are known to be allies. Dogs are simply faithful to whoever feeds them. Together with their owners, they believe that long walks are advantageous, that digging uncovers much, and that happiness brings on dancing – and that a growl can be better than a bite. But Benzi the blundering buffoon is a barker *and* a biter.

The canine yelped as he squeezed under the gate, and came lolloping into the paddock surrounding the stables, where he was never welcomed. His yapping disturbed the horses, and when he ventured near to sniff at any of them, they stamped and pored, and with tails swishing and ears pinned back and eyes widened, reared a hoof at him. The mongrel was quick to retreat, and cowered, and yelped again. But on this occasion he was pawing and nipping at something unusual - a beetle he had found. It was clawing, debilitated by insecticide and caught up in the strings and fabric of a discarded medical mask. The more it thrashed about, the more entangled it became. The weakening struggle enticed the canine. He nipped and snapped, and eventually crunched the coprophage. But the bitter taste of oozing insect-poison gave him a sneeze attack and, after repeatedly pounding the remains with both paws, he abandoned his plaything.

Kumburukah was in smithereens. The champ was chomped.

Any family, unbalanced in its many ways, will be pushed to redress the imbalance when there is an important change – such as a death. Dying is the concern of those left living, those who remain to ponder, as there is existence to be 'chewed over', if you like. Is the death of machismo, however, to be mourned or celebrated, when the fearsome become the frail, and the strong are made submissive, and the bully becomes the bullied? In the bundu, death knows no chief. Over the veld, the reward for wickedness is death. Across the savanna, what is appropriate and what is due, is called *zvakakodzera*. For coprophagi, it is dung-destiny, written in the rollings of manure.

As I scuffled around the chips of Kumburukah, I considered how I'd looked up to him, how I'd respected his rollings and admired his balls. There he lay: a mauled mound, a spread of splodge, a brother in bits. How much thicker is haemolymph than Dunghill Farm cattle poop, really? A life from the veld had come to the farm, and the thinking that is too consuming, kungufisiza, had barely followed.

But soon after I'd completed another dung-ball, a medium-sized attempt, hardly enough to be a manure-monument for my departed sibling, kungufisiza did come. The beetle can leave the bundu, but the bundu will return to bug the beetle. I knew how to bury dung-balls, and in a somewhat similar way, I had to let go of a brother who'd disowned me. There was no need to linger over anyone who had no interest in my being around. Had I ever wished him dead? *Had I?* I'd buried droppings a hundred times heavier than him, in a single night. Tolerating the intolerant is a dung-ball rolling downhill.

The distant Milky Way that always gives direction, was not gleaming and shimmering. The moon too was not full, but new. There are belief systems brought by humans from far-flung cultures over the oceans, with rituals and ceremonies, but none of them carry real comfort or understanding in the face of death. They have itemised analyses that bring order, but not hope: denial hatches into anger which develops into bargaining that pupaes into despair that metamorphoses into acquiescence. And from nearer-by: human descendants of those with the bundu in their blood, who have survived on the savanna for centuries, give gifts and kill cattle to feed the crying, and to give the deceased nourishment for the next metamorphosis in spirit. Wood is burned, and if the flame goes upwards to the Great Spirit Mwari, so will the deceased. The living are left behind, and they make music with mbiras to contact the ancestors, and perform ceremonies lest they incur the misfortunes of which the deceased is now free. And there is a final ritual one revolution of the earth later, when the spirit becomes a spirit guardian, and returns to protect the family.

Dung-balls are made to roll. Where there are piles of poop, there's manure to manage. If all dung-beetles were taken from the savanna, there would be no life. The farm with its cement-clad sheds and dust-spewing machines and humans, would die. The veld and its cycles of struggle would pass on. Kumbukurah, you were *something*. There's no right time to go, only time and life passing, and waiting for the stillness that brings enlightenment.

Chapter 23: Fighting

Beetles lose some, beetles win some. In the outcrops I'd given up home and hope, and on the farm I'd failed in a first-borne fight, and I'd lost a first-born sibling. On imbalance: my winning seemed clearly to be losing. Dung-ball building, one orb of ordure after the next, night in and night out – as my roller-instinct imposed – and securing my rollings some distance away, seemed pointless when there was so much manure going crusted. Where the bundu had been bare, the farm left feelers flush and coprophagi fed. The excremental excess of horses and cattle and sheep and pigs (not to delve into the seldom-selected and, of late, passed-over chicken waste, and the ideal but inaccessible human wasted wonders, of course) made me smug. I was full of myself, and full of dung.

Monotony invited rebellion, as it so often does, and Rollo ventured out looking for it. The density of dung-seekers gave plenty of opportunity for provocation. A dung-fight can always be unearthed and, to release some pent-up palpiness, Rollo soon hit upon a much smaller and weaker opponent. The contest was not even for a dung-ball although in his diminutive victory an undersized, hardly-formed glob of manure came Rollo's way, only to be pounced on, scrapped about and grabbed by two other underweight coprophagi. There had been a few side-kicks, half a wrestle, and a missed grab. For Rollo, it was a pathetic, not even a Pyrrhic, victory in poop.

I was ready for the next one. There were stag-skills to show-off, moves to pull off, and masculinity to assert. I had strength and speed to display, and guts and give to flaunt. I had dung-beetle dislodgings to do, and opponents to overturn. But when the real fight came, it was more of an untidy tussle. The nearest dweller, steadfast in the surrounding slush, needed – in my opinion – to budge or *be budged*. So I piled in. I pounced and prodded and pounded. Legs flaying and fighting, we rolled around in the roughage. Then my mandibles clenched, and I flipped my foe. He fled to a nearby pat, to groom and glare, hardly upset as he rapidly rebalanced himself, and in moments, he'd descended undamaged into the encircling dung. As if nothing of note had happened, *unogara*, a dweller-beetle, had unflappably re-positioned his palps in the poop, re-centred his clypeus – and sat re-established in excremental ease. There was no dung-ball for me to ride high on, to find orientation atop, and to stride away with. I'd come, I'd seen, I'd conquered – and there was no desire to dance.

Rollo retreated into the shadows of the dung-piles of disenchantment. He had not struggled for long enough in the veld to learn that victory gained through gratuitous violence is never worth the win. What would Stag, 'the onlooker', be doing had he witnessed this pointless display? Rollo waited, and searched for a stillness that did not come. Two bigger adversaries appeared however, and the air was soon clogged with interference.

Sonny and Benz, the young and the restless, had arrived. They glanced around for somewhere dung-free to sit, and settled in the shadows. The boy was tearful as he sat himself down, looking to his mobile phone for light and comfort. As he played on it, tiny coloured lights flashed around, and imperceptible signals made the insects nearby slightly more frenzied. Some flew further away, others nearer, while the dung-beetles continued toiling, with resistance. Meanwhile, the dog gambolled around, nipped at his own hindquarters, and scampered towards a nearby dung-beetle. He sniffed cautiously at it, flapped his ears, and retreated.

I beetled-off to find Stag. A friend in manure is a friend for sure. I'd assure him that I knew how to flip a foe. I'd also let him know that I'd gained a sense of whether I *needed* to fight or not... if he wasn't too busy 'hangin'' with his crowd. Then I paused, remembering that previously I'd left in swift selfishness, abandoning a friendship that was worth more than some new sense of outlandish pride. I'd argued with him when I should've listened and learned. Then I'd argued with myself – and learned. I'd discovered that dancing on a dung-ball was the way to find direction, not to show off that I'd lost myself. Being on top of the ball wasn't better than keeping it discreetly safe. I'd tell him that, fundamentally, I never had hostility in my haemolymph – the fighting was in my instinct, and not in my soul.

I'd grown under Stag's guidance and greatness. He was the father I never had. My dung-daddy. My mentor in manure. My mandibles may've been less mesmerizingly massive than his, and I may've been only half his height and a smidgeon of his size, and staggeringly un-stag-like – but my phallus was bigger than his. I was rising from follower to fighter to fornicator. The time was right for me to make the biggest dung-ball ever, and to find a female.

Chapter 24: Human Bonding

I am out observing the dung-beetles at the stables, again. Dunghill Farm is a fascinating place where nature is continuously, and inconspicuously, rearranging balance in an environment created by humans. There is a lot of horse, cow, sheep, pig and chicken manure confined to a few acres of farmyard. It has rained for the past three afternoons and the feed pens and open pigsties are watery and muddied, and no place for dung-beetle activity. At night, the horses are kept dry under cover where their droppings steam and stay damp, so coprophagi tend to congregate here. Dusk has just settled and the cycles of nocturnal activity are beginning. Dung-beetles are digging, feasting, balling and, I see over there, pairing off.

My note-taking is interrupted by barking – and Benz. I have not been overtly friendly towards him in my efforts to keep a distance between us. He is unhelpful in my observations, and something of a nuisance generally. I shine my torch directly in his eyes. He stops, a little way off, and stretches in his canine greeting posture. I ignore rather than welcome him, and he stays floored, tail wagging horse dung about. Then Sonny arrives, also unsure in his approach, armed with mobile phone and a packet of sweets. He sits near me, throws down the outer plastic and inner silver paper wrappings from a toffee that he pops into his mouth, and stares deliberately at his phone. It is quiet except for the sounds of horses' hooves scraping occasionally on cement floors and – I'm sure I can hear it – the buzz and rustle of dung-beetle activity. Sonny is teary-faced, and edges the packet of sweets towards me. I break the silence between us.

'Thanks, *Mwana*.' I try to make it sound as warm as possible.

'You're looking at the bugs again.' It was a statement and not an accusation this time. 'What's so interesting?'

'Come and see here.'

He seems eager to shift closer to me, but it is not near enough, or yet time, for me to put an arm around him. 'Dung-beetles can do so many things that people can't, and we're slowly learning how to understand them. They can see some colours outside the rainbow that we can't. They can communicate in ways that are too complicated for us to work out. They even use the stars to find their way home sometimes.'

Sonny tilts his head in suspicion, clutches onto another two sweets, and offers me one as a gift – already unwrapped. Then he reverts to the companionship and security of his phone.

'How come your phone works so well out here?' I'm thinking that perhaps an impersonal question will engage him in friendly conversation.

He is certainly more knowledgeable about cellular phones than I am. Once he gets going there is no stopping the flood of information about radio waves making digital voices, and EMFs and travelling at the speed of light. And why wi-fi is better than a service provider – even though his father disagrees. He shares more of his sweets as I tell him about how dung-beetles also use far-off connections, and have a kind of GPS to orientate themselves using the Milky Way. Sonny seems unconvinced but accepting. As I politely turn down his offer for another hurriedly unwrapped sweet, its papers strewn at our feet, I wonder whether bombarding him with dung-beetle research findings will engage him as much as his interest in cellular networking does. I smile at the irony of my looking for better connectivity.

'We have to be careful. Wi-fi radiation can be harmful to dung-beetles. It opens the calcium channels in certain cells which forces them to absorb more calcium ions. And this can cause a reaction in insects that interferes with their immune systems and their circadian – their day and night – rhythms. Plus, they may not be able to navigate too well, and their larvae and genes may be affected.' I was cantering along.

He was keeping up: 'So 5G will make things even worse?'

'Maybe for all of us,' I smiled meekly.

The large oak dining table seats six comfortably, but tonight's dinner is not an altogether comfortable occasion. Farmer Bertram, at the head, is an inflexible father, while Johanna maintains a sense of well-mannered formality that ensures that meals are incident-free. The children are in the company of 'grown-ups' so know that their conversations need to be in polite obedience. Dr Navors, 'Footie', seems to feel very at home in his brother-in-law's house. He is not an unusually large man, but he takes up a lot of space at the table. He leans over, smiles and brushes against me when we are all talking, and I feel less at ease than previously when he was not here.

The spread is hearty and generous. The home-grown vegetables are fresh and delicious, and every night roast meat is served – a chicken or sheep or cow that Joanna had arranged to be slaughtered earlier. Two days ago, I watched a carefully-selected sheep having its throat cut, being skinned, and hacked into manageable pieces. It was very efficiently done, but I had dung to explore.

'The kid's not eating all his food because he's having too many sweets,' Bertram remarks to his wife, 'and he left all the sweet papers littering the stables. Near where I also found one of his school medical masks in the mud.' The father speaks as if the boy is not there.

'Sissie, please pass the gravy to your Uncle Footie,' Johanna says.

The men are out on the verandah smoking and talking about how the day went. There is a sizeable pot of coffee to drink, and medical advice to be given and taken. Jo and I are in Sissie's bedroom, tucking her in for the night. She is a sweet and obliging girl, all innocence, and unsure at this stage of what to make of her life.

'I think it's Rana's turn tonight,' Jo edges me smilingly into the position of telling the bedtime story – for both of them, as well as for Sonny who has crept in to join us. As a child I always went to bed by myself, so have no real repertoire of tales to draw from.

'Once upon a time…' I know how they begin, but I am fumbling, and to avoid disappointing the three attentive Hidebounds, I turn a well-documented Australian scientific dung-beetle research trip into a (kind of) bedtime story. It is (relatively) 'long ago', in the 1960s, and the threatening 'baddie' is a dung-disaster the country was facing at that time. 'The native dung-beetles that fed on the hard kangaroo droppings were not eating the soft pats left by cows that had been imported from far, far away. So the farmlands became covered in dung, and the bad, horrible bush-flies multiplied and multiplied until they were completely out of control.' I try to keep it interesting – there is no fairy tale magic (except the marvels of nature) and no heroes or heroines (except for the beetles). 'The Australian Dung Beetle Project was started by some very caring and important scientists and doctors, and over 50 types of dung-beetles from all over the world were introduced. And soon' – drama… tragedy averted 'the new dung-beetles got busy on all the dung, and the dung-piles were beaten back, and bush-fly numbers dropped by over 90 percent.' There is no wedding for a proper fairy tale finish, so I end my story explaining how the balance of nature was restored and that all the farmers lived 'happily ever after'.

I look around, and see that my audience has grown: Farmer Bertram is listening at the door, and as soon as the happy ending is pronounced, he taps Sonny on the shoulder, and the boy is summarily dismissed, and follows his father down the passage.

'The experiment was so successful that other places in Australia repeated it.' Dr Futiel Navors pokes his head into the doorway, and peers in at me. 'And in New Zealand too!'

I slept well last night thinking about how my storytelling skills could prove useful when the time came for my report back assessment lecture next month. Dry facts woven into a bedtime narrative… who would have thought it reasonable? I allow myself to feel some pride in the probability that Johanna and the children are warming to me. I chuckle – or is it sneer? – recalling the image of Dr 'Footie' Navors in the shadows between the door posts, not unlike the cows that he has immobilized in the crush to minimize danger or risk of injury.

Tonight the full moon is outshining the stars. The uncovered lightbulbs hanging at the corners of the shed are swarming with insects. After this afternoon's cloudburst, the rainwater has mostly drained away, or has left small, hoofmark-shaped puddles of watery dung. It is a perfect night to start writing in the new notebook from '*Your new friend, Jo*'. As I turn my attention to the fascinating dung-beetles around the outlet that drains from the pigsties, I hear Sonny and Sissie calling.

'Wiwi! Wiwi, where are you?'

Young Mwana sees me and he takes his sister's hand, and they jog in my direction. They are without their phones and, oblivious of the farm odours, are busily scoffing yoghurt from small plastic tubs using bright plastic spoons. When Sissy finishes scraping her tub with her spoon clean-licked, she unthinkingly drops them into the drain, and asks, 'Please, Miss Rana, can I have a special name too?'

Sonny picks them up and, rather neatly, stacks her empty tub into his.

'We should go and pick up the sweet papers at the stables.' He is a little hesitant. 'Will you come with us, Wiwi?'

'Of course I will, Mwana.'

We walk hand-in-hand, the three of us swinging arms in the bright moonlight, and a horse nickers as we pass by. It is a gentle, breathy whinny.

'It's a greeting,' Sonny informs me, proud in his ability to interpret. The young man is strangely happy as he looks around for sweet papers, and each time he picks one up, turns to look at me as if I were a supervisor waiting to commend him.

'Look at all these worms in the poop,' Sissie says. Perhaps, she is learning how to study dung too.

The three of us are a close trio of observers hunched over some hardening horse droppings, and Sonny uncovers a bulbous white dung-beetle larva. Sissie is clearly unimpressed and takes a step back in trepidation. I start talking about metamorphosis – telling the story of a dung-beetle's life, and how everything depends on the dung. Sonny is not listening to the details. I think my voice has lulled young Mwana into a gentle peace.

'Do people have meta-morn-aphis?' he asks.

'We have birthdays instead, Mwana.'

'So, *can* I?' Sissie asks again, almost in prayer. I open my mouth and take some moments to think about a name for her.

'How do you like *Runako*?'

She folds her arms and, without caring what it means or where she sits, her little moon-face beams.

'It means you are *beautiful*.'

Sonny is so pleased for his sister, Runako, he joins her in the dirt.

'And you are not Mwana any more,' I tell Sonny, sweet papers and yoghurt tubs in one hand, younger sister in the other, and eyes cleared of tears, 'You are my *Murume*.'

Chapter 25: Preparing

It is an instinct naturally acknowleged, that a single beetle in possession of some good balls, must be rolling in want of a mate. Whether driven by impulse or aedeagus, the male rises in search of another of his species. In communication, and when the exuded chemistry is correct, he is able to recognize and be stimulated by the need for toil. There is both 'u' and 'i' in 'building'. So, for a dung-beetle, shaping a dung-ball is not merely an act of repetition, but a habit, which gives birth to excellence.

I sat half-buried and semi-emergent between a dropping and a hard pat. With my inflatable endophallus exposed and its chitinous sclerites showing, I was surely a dung-beetle of desire. I'd built dung-balls and fought dung-battles. I'd rolled and wrestled. I oozed moist machismo and claggy confidence – yet remained unnoticed. There were hordes of beetles about, and many passing by, mostly bigger and more often female, some a shade inquisitive – but none captivated by my confidence or enraptured in my eroticism. Were my chemical outpourings merely lacklustre leaks? And what were all these passer-by-beetles making of my mouthpart-scrapings and leg-rubbings? I sat unrecognized and deflated. I had no balls with which to brag, no dung-balls of deserving dimension, and no reputation with which to truly roll. I was, once again, nothing special enough, nowhere near to even next to best.

Rollo, not on a roll, crouched in sedentary stillness for some time. Then, as he had done before, he lifted himself out of the manure and, rising from the dung, emerged to a place of relative clarity. With pupation two months in the past, and experience on his side, he reassessed. He was learning that when all else fails: philosophise! He recognised the futility of the aggression that comes from a need to be noticed, and he repressed his rage. He lowered his thorax, and returned to the faecal matter. He knew to use what he had, to get his dung together to tumble in triumph. He had proven the pointlessness of macho posturing, and was ready to be a reasonable *Rollo*.

The readiness is all, but success takes structuring and toil. Any mate worth his weight makes it great. So, I thought I'd bring Stag's hugely impressive dung-ball, to be noticed and attract admiration, but when I orienteered back to where I had (mostly) buried it, all I found was a dried and deflated daub of dung. It was flat and ugly, and obviously past its roll-by date. It was a messy message that food-balls had to give way to brood-balls. I was no longer rolling for myself. There came a sense of unbalancing that pushed me into a larger realization of deeper labours ahead. There were flashes of losing individuality and of having to conform, for approval, to nourish future growing larvae and, ultimately, for the sake of dung-beetledom.

I scuttled and searched, and found a small wad of shrubs, grazed down to a clump of sturdy stems, where I hollowed out a pit in the sand. I'd build an entire nest of dung balls and show her: I may be an outsider from the outcrops, and have come from a lesser dung-pile in the veld, but bundu-beetles were breedworthy – and when she sees my balls, she'll want the whole hotbed! I toiled through the night, ignoring the distractions of hound and humans, and rolled 'til the morning, and shaped the sturdiest stronghold. Not only was my brain the size of a grain of grit, but I'd built the best brooding chambers. There was ball-room for generations. I'd prepared a palace – a *paradise* – for a partner in poop!

And my final and finest brood-ball was shaped in skill and patted to perfection. It was an extraordinary orb of excrement, soft and solid, full-flavoured and life-giving. I sprang onto it and – there was no time for savanna stillness – released a long-repressed female-fetching flow of pheromone.

Chapter 26: Pairing

It is another truth naturally acknowledged, that if a female likes what she sees, she may hop onto a dung-ball and be taken for the ride of her life. As the female in focus sensed Rollo's behaviour-changing agent, his floods of pheromone, her feelers twitched, and her enthralled instinct propelled her towards him. As he mounted his temptation-ball, she was enticed, femurs flapping, and trembling at the trochanters, to join him – just as another inquisitive insect, a potential suitor perhaps, moved nearby, and came in a little too close for contentment.

With one full-cut and a ball-change and a well-centred side-kick, I spurred the intruder. We writhed and wrestled. Fortunately, the tussle was fleeting and, with the ball rolling in my favour, challenge and challenger were briskly dismissed and overturned. With my palps in possession of the poop-prize, there was no impeding this front-running roller headed, backwards, as I drove my dung-ball of devotion to the clump of shrub stems guarding my hotbed of rollings. And when Mukadzi, the female procured, took to rallying around, and began helping me bury the orb of lure-manure, my pantry of prepared poop became a brood-ball boudoir.

No creatures, with the exception of homo sapiens, sense a need to create concepts or judgements of beauty. Pairing is purely for the purpose of continuing the species; so choosing a mate, naturally, is a matter of broodworthiness and breedability, not beauteousness. 'Loveliness' is an absurdity. 'Pretty' serves no purpose. 'Fair' is foul, and only 'fit' is fitting. To seek a partner who is well-formed and proportioned – even statuesque – elicits a far more favourable return. The beauty is in the *size* of the beheld. Sensing surpasses 'sensual'. Sexual out-smarts 'sexy'. In the deep veld wisdom of the savanna – and on the farm too – *natural* selection ensures the survival of the fittest.

It was attachment at first scent. She was dungalicious, and smelt perfectly of poop. She was sticky and slimy on the sides, with vertex connected to the pronotum connected to the elytra, in attracting alignment with a centred scutellum in – to be sure – serviceable shape. She was hard-shelled, and grooved at very regular intervals. When she opened her wings, the lady-bug lured! I leered at her legs, twelve fetching femurs, tibias and tarsi designed to shape, and claws clammy with excrement. And a prime posterior pygidium! My reward, my *runako*!

We really rolled together. Where the dung was delicious, we dined, and dug it. Where the poop was plentiful, we piled dung-ball upon brood-ball. Partnered, we rose to challengers that were tough, and sometimes managed to take off with their efforts. We satisfied ourselves in satisfying each other. I taught her the meaning of *tanaka*: the good times in the savanna that come after struggle and hardship. And she taught me how to dance.

Despite her glimmer of greenness, sheltered past, and inexperience as an insect, Mukadzi knew how to be patient and firm. When choreographing, she often fidgeted and fretted over Rollo's three pairs of 'left feet'. He, on the other hand, found her basic five positions anything but basic. He would bend his back legs too readily, as though he preferred to be sitting; and straighten his forelegs too much, as though spinning and street dancing, or engaged in unarmed combat. His pliés in poop were pitiful, his etendrés in excrement awful. His pirouettes flew in the face of precision; he slid where he was meant to shift, and his leg transitions were pointless. His tarsi would not tourner, nor would his femurs relever; and there was no maintaining any proper turnout. His efforts were indirect, unsustained and heavy, and Mukadzi had her claws full avoiding his spurs.

I'd achieved less than simply shaking a leg or six. I tried to sway her way but Mukadzi's moves were exacting, and it seemed she pointedly performed pirouettes at me, with a precision and possession that I failed to follow. I could assimilate some attitudes but couldn't dance her dance. She had hard-work in her haemolymph, and was a beetle beetle-burning too bright in the stables every night. In comparison, I was too seldom on my toes, and stepped down as my instinct reminded me that I was intrinsically an indolent insect, an individual that preferred passivity, and our differences were underscored. Even the emission of pheromones took more exertion, and I feelered a future when they would flow less freely, and more faintly. Would the duty-filled days of endless dung-balling lull us into a stupor of indifference, and dim our ideals? Perhaps we'd drift further and further away from the stillness that brings peace, where life begins.

Chapter 27: Mounting

'Let's go then, you and I, when the evening is spread out against the sky, like an overturned stag-beetle. Our brood-balls are stacked up, and we've danced together in dung: let's do it!'

In the many dances of discovery and processes that pre-empt procreation, Rollo was developing some grasp of having to shift his sensings from his aedeagus to his instinct. The dung-rolling swain had gathered a mostly appropriate mate, and with further pheromones to send forth, had farther functions to perform. He sensibly selected early evening, a cooler time of the day, when the farm air was thicker with humidity, and the wind had died down, to defecate, body tilted sideways and abdomen lifted upward, and fart his final mind-altering substances at his female.

She, in synchronicity, had satisfied her sensings with my adequate balls. She'd tallied my talents, perceived what poop I could scoop, and seen the dung I could deliver. She'd uncovered method in my manure, and was well-pleased by my piles. My mandibles resembled prize pincers, and I had spurs that shone of sludge – she'd certainly noticed. Most prominently though, I was a *tumbler*: precisely her type!

Dung-beetle fornication is a brief burst, functional and, in contrast to homo sapien mating, is never just for 'fun'. Front legs armed with serrations for gripping stability, and all feelers aligned and dampened, the participants appear prepared. Insect intercourse is neither indulgent, nor is the process of reproduction in any way recreational. Sperm packets are passed via the male's inflatable endophallus which is lined with chininous sclerites for traction, into the female's genital tract. Her primary vagina has a single sclerotized portion that supports her bursa, and her infundibulum positioned at right angles to this, runs into the spermathecal duct that is attached to the annular spermathecal where the received semen is stored.

Copulation complete – my job was done! I'd swept my front tibiae over her shiny thorax, and, half-mounted, turned her around, scraped across her moistened elytra causing her to lift her abdomen, and entered her. After some stirrings, she stepped forward, and I was pushed back. I re-set the operation by further scrapings across her thorax, and when they were reciprocated, I re-ascended and, lest she abandoned me in my piles of poop, or found me incapable of prolonged copula stimulation, I held on, and stayed – in a *new* dance position – on top.

Dung-beetles prefer to have sex underground or at least semi-submerged in dung: the earth *always* moves for them. Copulation is a costly activity and uses up important bodily resources of water and energy; and some insects can lose up to a quarter of their body weight in ejaculate. Rollo was seemingly too sapped to seek out other females to bring to his pile of brood-balls, so he dismounted and stayed to watch over his mate. She could decide to find other males and seek out sperm competition, particularly if she instinctively sensed that his body size, or prolonged copula stimulation, were second-best. So, to ensure she did not roam, he re-mounted, re-entered – and then relaxed. Rollo remembered he also had his dung-pile to defend, and kept watch, without looking for trouble. He had to ensure that soon he would be in paternal attendance, adding his final touches to the masterpiece brood-ball in which Mukadzi would lay their first egg.

Chapter 28: Human Feeling

This evening seems particularly restful. The cicadas that screeched in the leafy msasa trees at the side of the garden at dusk have quietened earlier than usual. Around the sheds and stables there is a stillness, eerie and peaceful, as if I was miles away from the farm, and near the rocky outcrops to the north. I took a long walk there yesterday afternoon, across the recently burned fire-guards, to clear my mind.

I was a city-slicker out in the bundu. There were holes in the ground that were obviously burrows, now deserted and blocked with tangled, old knotted spiderwebs. I noticed signs of beetle activity here and there, remnants of dung-balls under one of the jutting rocky ledges, but I guessed that the lack of wildlife, and hence manure, had driven their numbers down. I put away my notebook. I did not live in this world but understood then that I lived in many. The small weather-rounded stones were shapes of time and, as a slight breeze blew, I felt embraced, and content to be by myself. Well-learned scientific principles and proofs that always brought assurance receded, as a simpler solitude warmed me. I noticed a duiker looking up from behind a distant tree – it had been there all the time, alert and chewing. My floating thoughts were interrupted by an insistent fly, and a lizard appeared on a distant rocky ledge, watching. I was not alone.

Then a loud, sharp crack rang out across the veld. Then another. And a third. The booming gunshots overtook each other, echoed outward, then diminished, to be followed by the loud voices of men, and a madly yelping dog. I was shocked and frightened – and then ashamedly relieved – to recognize the shouts of Bertram and Dr Navors as the men trod across the landscape, cursing, and disappeared out of sight beyond the treeline. The stillness returned.

The family ate a hearty dinner last night. Vegetables from Johanna's garden complimented the whole chicken that had been roasted for our consumption. As I finished nibbling at my drumstick, I realized that if I faced Dr Navors directly, I could see, out of the corner of my eye, the line of animal skulls that hung on the inside wall of the verandah: decorations of mounted buffalo horns and spiraling kudu horns and duiker prongs, all jutting from bleached white skulls with big round bone sockets where the eyes once were.

'Looking for something?' He ogled me.

The bluntness of Dr Navors' words jolted everyone into a momentary silence. Then the children glanced around for whatever they were not supposed to be seeing. Johanna reminded her husband that his serviette had fallen onto the floor. And I filled the emptiness with safe, beetle information.

'Beetles can see different wavelengths. Their sight is called photoreception and different parts of their eyes perceive different colours.'

'Strawberries, everyone?' Johanna was serving dessert. 'There's fresh cream in the mauve jug.'

'For example, they can't see red. But they can see ultraviolet rays - which people can't see.' I had managed not to repeat 'different'.

When the tappings and scrapings of dessert spoons on empty plates settled, I continued.

'We have single-lens eyes while some insects have about twenty-five thousand or more per eye.' Sonny was duly impressed by the large number. 'So it must be like looking through gauze,' and for Farmer Bertram's sake, 'or a woven-wire fence.'

'Or a tea strainer,' interjected Joanna heartily as she began serving the after-dinner tea and coffee.

'Actually, some people use yellow lights outside because the insects can't see yellows and oranges so well. And you can use UV lights to lure night-flying insects to electric grids or traps... '.

'Zap!' exclaimed Sonny, slapping his palms together. 'We have them at school.'

'Next week we have to burn some more fire-guards. Maybe, if the bandage is off your leg, you want to come – and help?' Johanna stole a glance at Bertram as he said this, and then, to soften the blow or the heighten the invitation – by reverting to facts and supportive information – continued, 'If you burn the dry grass and make strips of clear land, then bushfires won't spread out of control. You have to make fires to stop fires. Every year. To keep the farm safe. So if I decide to sell it one day, buyers will know it's well looked-after.'

The word 'sell' echoed around the room. Johanna, always meticulous in her wifely duties, knocked the lid off the coffee-pot. Dr Navors choked on a mouthful of tea. Clearly the subject had not been broached before, or appropriately, until now.

'Nobody knows what will happen to this country in the future. There's not a lot of good news in politics these days. What do *you* think, Miss *Kuwiwirana*?'

When it was time for the children to be in bed, I popped into Sonny's room to see how his knee was. It was freshly bandaged, and blood-free. He told me he'd been pushed onto a rough cement floor at school but was not keen to talk about it. There was also a bruise at the back of his neck, which I stroked gently, just to let him know that I had seen it.

119

'We have to take good care of ourselves. We don't have hard, waterproof exoskeletons,' I said smilingly as his eyes welled-up in appreciation, 'we are not dung-beetles.'

As I retired to my bedroom, Dr Navors was loitering in the passage, blocking my way. His shirt was spattered with coffee, but his confidence was unsoiled.

'Yes,' he smirked, and turning himself a little to let me past, shirt unbuttoned and arms in an open cattle-crush position, 'we have to take care of each other. Nice exoskeleton, Rana.'

My thoughts are broken by the sounds of a pig-fight. Not the usual murmurs and oinks and grunts, but snarls and roars and howls. Bertram had put some boars together in the open pig-pens this afternoon, and perhaps they are competing for dominance. Near to where I am, as always, seated, even the horses are alerted. But it is momentary, and they soon turn back to chewing straw, knowing – I suppose – that it is not their struggle. Mostly, I feel grateful that there is always enough dung and beetle activity to focus on, and to launch me towards halfway through filling my second note book, the gift from Jo.

Bertram strides out towards the hullabaloo in the pig sties. He is pointing a rifle and looks well-prepared to shoot at anything troublesome. Sonny is a little way behind, inquisitive but reticent. He looks afraid. Bertram shouts at the pigs, and their noises soon die down. Then, rifle uncocked, he approaches me.

'I've had a good offer for the farm.' He looks out, past the stables and pigsties and feed-pens that he has built. 'But where would we go? And what about Johanna? And the kids.'

There is nothing I can say. It is hardly my business. Sonny comes to stand next to his step-father and they seem to be waiting for my response. I am seeing two little lost boys, and there are no helpful beetle facts and figures coming to mind.

'Murume, remember I'm taking you to school in the morning. Have you got that dung-beetle ready for your nature study talk tomorrow?'

Chapter 29: Procreating

Once the copulation was complete, and before Rollo had fully recovered, Mukadzi's fast-working mouth-parts began hollowing out a chamber in the dung-ball she had selected in which to lay an egg. Then, with her mate observing fairly closely, she defecated on the chamber walls, and inserted her tubular-shaped ovipositor, with its three pairs of appendages, into the opening, to prepare a place for the egg, to transmit it, and then to place it, most suitably, near the upper, angular part of the brood-ball interior, at the newly-created air-intake vent. She proceeded to close the chamber, deposit and smear a layer of soil over the opening, and then ascended the smooth, moist ball, and twitched at her onlooking mate.

She was my fertile female, and a beetle of breeding. A conscientious coprophage, and my insect of change – my *dung-ee*. She was a fecund transformer, a converter who turned our food-balls into brood-balls. As mates, we minded our manure, somewhat mutually, and I partnered her at the balls where we'd dally – and I'd dutifully dance her steps. Together we pressed, and I was always egged-on. Half-burying our first formation, we worked overhead for the zygote to enlarge and the yolk grains to grow. Above all, we tramped, and tread down encouragement for embryonic emergence. Then we were onto the second brood-ball, a third, and others after that – each an exhausting incubation.

I slogged in that slush to sire siblings of quality as well as equality. I'd lived through the drawbacks and disadvantages of being poorly-placed, and I was almost as diligent as she was to ensure each brood-ball was perfectly tended, and each egg had the opportunity to emerge as an unusually gifted larva, with every chance of becoming a champion coprophage. The parental protection that scurried and hovered over my early metamorphoses had extended deep into dung. A caring parent *does* make a vital difference. Remembering how those maternal scrapes had kept my head up, I knew to pass down paternal pats of importance, such as I'd not known, to our emerging offspring.

Mukadzi was a heedful mother and, as Rollo had turned from the veld to the farm, and transmuted and metamorphosed into fatherhood, she too turned from Mukadzi to become 'Layla'. She was an egg-depositor of distinction, always on the lookout for fresh shelters best for brood-balls in which to lay her *zai*. She knew which spots around the stables were wet but not watery, which areas of the feed-pens were too sandy and would dry out easily, and where the ground around the pig-enclosure had a higher clay content so never became soggy, and would form a protective crust, and keep brood-balls moist and alive. She laid where she knew how the contents of the brood-balls would sustain the larvae, and affect their growth, and judiciously selected dung-balls that contained the right balance of undigested plant and meal matter, rich in gut minerals, and wrapping a sensible amount of roughage. Without excessive palp-prodding, she could deduce dung-desirability from the hues of the freshly-exposed manure as it turned from greenish to blackening in the atmosphere. And she knew to lay her *zai* some distance from where the homo sapiens – the adult female with her staring eyes and prodding and poking claws, and the young male with his incessant voicings and questionings – perched.

Over the days that rolled by, the brood-balls became rougher, covered by the small pellets of faeces produced by the larva so dependent on the quality of Rollo and Layla's rollings. Soon would come the stillness of pupation; and then, after one full cycle of the moon, it would be revealed which brood-balls supported instars that had lived through the larval challenges, past the inaction and imposed independence of pupation, and they would emerge as adult dung-beetles.

In the farmyard *kungufisiza* – where there was never stillness – there was much to chew over. I ruminated regularly in the excesses of Dunghill doings. In the *zai* that I'd fertilized, and the *mhezi* that were metamorphosing, lay the stirring beginnings of a new generation: mine. These deliberations in dung, these contemplations of *kungufisiza,* were the new dance moves. I didn't need to be rolling all the time, endlessly shoveling and slapping, and sculpting and guarding – always guarding. There were times to loosen up too, and to let go, to make openings for perception and occasions for insight – *opportunities.* When you've rolled a dung-ball that someone else is eating, you have a hold on life.

Surrounded by scurrying coprophagi, Rollo sat senselessly on a horse's heap of half-digested hay. Becoming a father had afforded him the right to listen less, or so it seemed, and he had eased into reckless disregard and casual carelessness. He never noticed the human hand that hoisted him horse-hock high, almost as though in flight, but *clenched.*

Chapter 30: Colliding

Midway upon the journey of our lives, we may find ourselves within a strongbox dark, for the straightforward pathway has been lost. Rollo spent much of the day, in a cardboard shoebox, like an incarcerated pupa, far from any stillness, and was transported to places unknown. There were punched-in holes in the lid and sides of the echoing container, spiracle-like to let in air, supposedly, and through which light beamed as though the Milky Way had been jammed uncomfortably and pointlessly close. Most of the time he spent helplessly chirping and squeaking, and thrashing about and frantically waggling. He was held aloft and inspected, gawked and laughed at, and occasionally used as a clawing monster to scare shrieking schoolgirls.

There were sounds and smells he had never sensed before. *Homo Sapiens* spoke out and were silent; they sang and recited, and throughout the day there was a loud bell that clanged with fearful regularity. Halfway through the morning, after a particularly long resounding and reechoing of the alarm, he was taken to a set of large cubicles where only younger male humans congregated, and he recognized the heady, inviting aroma of omnivore excrement. But he was too disturbed, too far from the familiarities of Layla and his fast-evolving family, to feel hungry, and continued trying to claw his way sliding down the ungraspable walls of his cruel cardboard cocoon. This was life on the other side of the River Mubundovi.

Again, I heard the gratings and beatings of steel. I sensed the aromas of burning fuels, and the vibrations and bumps of mechanical movement. The walls hemming me in jolted and repositioned repeatedly, but I remained on my feet, mostly, tarsi sliding but pronotum-prone. The clashings of *kungufusiza* and cogitation too, were fiercely unsettling. After some time, the bouncing around abated, the shudderings ceased, and I recognized the welcome screeches of late-afternoon cicadas. And there were woofings and yelpings and sniffings, a bump and a thud, and then the familiar, half-homely smells of Dunghill Farm gusted around me. The covering above me had shifted, and I flew out quickly towards the nearest square of sunlight, hitting into a solid semi-visible obstruction, and was smacked to the ground. I scuttled across the lifeless skin of a sheep, and fluttered past the stark-white heads of long-dead veld creatures, and took wing into the dizzying afternoon heat. In confusion, I circled and soared, and buzzed and whirred. No longer confined, I flitted into the open air, then swerved earthwards, and collapsed onto a pile of dead and decaying leaves. I slunk in speedily, and lingered under cover to regain some energy, and to wait for darkness and the Milky Way to guide me home.

Rollo had found his way onto the Dunghill gardens compost pit, a sizeable rectangular hole dug into the ground, a short flight downwind from the vegetable patch. Garden foliage, uprooted weeds, and human food scraps and leftovers were thrown there, and then smothered with sheep manure dug out from building up in layers inside the kraal, covered in soil,

127

and left to decompose into farm-made fertilizer. The rotting contents, not having passed through any living duodenal systems, were of no nutritional interest to Rollo. As he crawled under a head of decaying, maggot-infested cabbage, he contemplated his place in the world.

Were the same, or similar – or even different – creatures meant to exist together on earth? The Hidebound family had developed a farm, a working environment, where humans, animals, birds, insects and plants survived alongside, even depended, on each other. Rollo had disowned his sibling Kumburukah, yet connected with the outlandish alien Stag. And were there places in the great savanna where rivers and walls divided lives and separated souls? Would Layla welcome Rollo back sensing that he had not merely meandered off, as he had done on too many occasions in the past? Where in this planet of plenty could acceptance reside? What comfort could be found in *kungufisiza*?

Insects have instincts. We don't need the complications that come from long narrative communications, so Layla heard nothing of my adventures. She was laboring as always, but surely sensed odours on me that were very foreign. I reeked of exploits from over the river, yet she continued as though she'd not detected my absence: had I been such a neglectful father? She was a marvelous mother, and certainly a finer parent, and overseer, than I was. Very little dung hardened around her. Most likely, she *did* notice, and she was maintaining a maternal stillness. Her female disregard could deflate any conflict – then there'd be no confrontation. I couldn't dance her dance, and I was fresh out of pheromones to flaunt.

I wasn't out looking for another mate, definitely. Why chase something not as good as you have? There was nothing savanna-wide as hard-working and sperm-receiving and egg-producing as Layla. Could I only learn the value of something when it was gone? In another revolution of the moon most of our offspring would've flown off. That day of journeying across the river, those hours of agonising extraordinariness, were past. A new moon was beaming, and there was no better time to leave the old and make unmediated contact with the new, with the moment-by-moment mystery of the unsure. There are some misunderstandings that exceed *kungufusiza* – they transcend the call for resolution. For insects, peace is preferable to conflict. Both farm and veld are full of controlling misconnections, and I didn't need to bring bundu burdens to the brood-chambers of my mindful mate. There *is* a right time, far from the rules of the savanna, and there's time passing too – and I was driven to look ahead, and rolled on.

Even before the entire compost pit had been covered in sheep droppings, the details of any disagreement Layla and I could've faced, had faded into insignificance, or decomposed into indifference. But – for me – the *reasons* for the conflict were clarified. It was a farm foofaraw, in which I was, unusually, not wrong; and she was, as usual, kind. In some moments of strange stillness, becoming sensitised to this, and knowing what it was to be contained in a strongbox, and to be lost, I tallied my pheromones, and rolled some more dung.

Chapter 31: Human Opportuning

It is the day of my departure from Dunghill Farm. Jo and I are sitting on the polished cement-floored verandah that extends halfway around the house, sharing mid-morning tea. Rusk-dunking has become a comforting ritual that we enjoy together, and that now complements our conversations. Sonny and Sissie are sitting on the verandah wall, mostly silent and smiling, unsure of how to respond to this, our last, gathering. Farmer Bertram soon joins us. He normally comes to the house only for meals as he has a coffee flask that is his companion, that he makes sure accompanies him, around the farm. I am touched that he is here to see me off, and he takes me on one last, quick farmyard walkabout. Of course, I am very familiar with the sheds, and sties and stables, and he leads me, somewhat directly, to my favourite spot, on the crumbling wall, overlooking the spread of his horses' manure.

'They never stop working,' he remarks, 'Not the horses, I mean – the insects,' he quips, finding solace in a little intended humour.

'No, it's not in their haemolymph.' We smile, and for the first time my beetle-facts seem appropriate. 'Thanks for everything, Bert, for all the opportunities. I learned a lot.' I smile again. His name is so easy to say.

'I can build a farm. But a family – that's... '. He sniggers, as he points at a pair of dung-beetles battling over a dung-ball. Then he stands up and, casting a farmer's eye over the newly-stocked feed pens, says amicably, 'You're welcome, Miss Kuwiwirana. Thank *you*.'

We amble back to the verandah, past the fowl run where I notice, for the first time some spotted guinea-fowl, with their variegated chicks, pecking around amongst the other brown and white hens. A large rooster stops scratching in the dirt, inspects us, and muffles a squawk.

My large suitcase has been brought out, and Sissie has left a small hand-coloured note and posy on it. She accompanies me to the bedroom to fetch my briefcase and tote bag. I give her my fashionable handbag to help carry out, and she beams, gliding ladylike over the cow-skin carpets, to the front door.

As we pass along the passage, I say goodbye to the old woman in black in the corner. She is, as always, clicking and chewing at her dentures, hands shuffling about a crochet hook and wool, hardly looks up, and leaves the parting impression of a ruminating dung-beetle. The trophy animal skulls along the verandah wall

131

glare, and hang lined up as if to bid me a formal farewell. My car has been washed and cleaned of the spatterings of black berries dropped from the wild waterberry tree under which I have been parked these past weeks, and its battery is fully charged. I rev up easily, and the Hidebounds' goodbyes and remarks of appreciation seem more pronounced than mine.

Sonny is at the end of the lawn holding open the security gate as I drive through. My last view of the white homestead is with Murume, my sentinel, gently waving his mobile phone, and holding Benzi firmly by the collar.

I notice too, thickets of wild zinnias – noxious weeds to farmers – flowering along the roadside. There are no other vehicles on the farm road, and the gates have all been opened, so the dust my car wheels churns up stays comfortably behind me. As I turn onto the highway, and drive past the *Mubundovi River ~ Caution* signpost and over the bridge, I turn up my music, and head on home.

Nine months have whizzed by since I left the farm, and my thesis on dung-beetle activity is complete. I graduated with scores in areas that directed me away from veterinary science and more towards integrated studies. I am working busily, though not always confidently, in new academic directions, exploring common ground between medicine and sociology and philosophy, trying to make sense of today, and how and where we live. There are posters plastered on trees and buildings all around the university campus, and my unusual academic focus has created a noticeable amount of internet buzz. There are members of the university council, and concerned parties further afield, that believe in new directions in 'humane' and affirmative academic pursuits, and who have been generous in providing grants and scholarship support. Of course, there are also doubters and cynics.

The countdown to the live internet webcasting from the centrally-located and aptly-selected General Purpose Hall has begun. A range of university departments have sent staff to investigate my findings. For a lunchtime lecture, and a relatively inexperienced speaker, the venue is remarkably full. Very soon, the technicians are thumbs-up. We enter formally. There is applause. I hardly hear the wordy introduction, and somewhere between determination and panic, I launch 'OPPORTUNING'.

The presentation went well, I think, but it will take some time and feedback, and winding-down, for me to make a balanced assessment. I had been candid without seeking confrontation, stuck my neck out and, unlike a Dunghill Farm slaughter-designated sheep, I am alive. After hours of persistent practice, I was able to present in semi-automatic mode, in order to be more alert to audience response. I started in safety, with the facts and figures of the five thousand different species of dung-beetle, the more than two thousand in the family

Scarabaeidae with over seven hundred in our region, and the one hundred and fifty of the genus *Catharsius,* meaning 'purifier', which may be found in our immediate environment. As I looked out at the audience I saw a swarming mass of similarly-masked, diverse-looking creatures – very dung-beetle-like – here to inspect and, hopefully, digest my discharges. When I described the stables of dung, my rural research environment, as a microcosm in stark contrast to current society, I noticed Bertram and Johanna, respectfully dressed-up for their trip to the city and to a university lecture, and wondered how they would deal with their lives being paralleled to manure-eating insects. Dr Futiel 'Footie' Navors, more casually attired, was sitting next to Jo, his sister, but once my discussion of how male dung-beetles often leave to find other mates soon after coupling, attempted or successful, he had exited. Bertram looked like an obedient schoolboy, intently attentive, as I explained how utilitarianism, which is a human construct promoting happiness, that actually makes us unhappy, differed from my new concept and the focal point of the lecture: *'opportuning'*. A few latecomers were peering around the entrance doors as I was highlighting the need for us all to metamorphose so that opportunities are made available for others. Throughout the lecture, Jo kept herself occupied taking notes, looking up and lowering pen and notebook to clap firmly every time anyone else did. There were other stirrings of agreement, or discontent, as I progressed into explaining the philosophy of *opportuning*, that is was not in any way an enemy of excellence, but was about 'finding direction', as dung-beetles do using the Milky Way which they recognize not as an unreachable collection of stars but as a means to a map. Some listeners found this idea far-fetched, while others, including Bertram, eventually, flinched when I power-pointed research statistics indicating the parallels in the prevalence of homosexuality in insects and humans.

A cell phone rang in the auditorium, and the owner was quick to fumble it into silent mode. This seemed an appropriate – and unplanned – time to chat a little about the harm done to everyone, humans included, by mobile phone and wi-fi radiation, and to tell how insects' magnetic fields and genetic material and immune systems and systems of navigation and day and night cycles were affected. To avoid further ramblings, I reverted to my prepared, rehearsed lecture notes, and progressed onto what I considered the most significant area of opportuning: death.

'Of course I realise that I'm not experienced in death,' I began, and a murmuring of laughter confirmed that there were still people attentive. 'It's like a river, just a small stream really, that needs crossing. Merely a process. Hardly a change. Time passing, not past.' The elderly Theology Department representative leered forward, 'Not an opportunity to grieve over,' and cuddled his clerical collar, 'just an *opportuning*.' He seemed further discomforted as I pointed out that only human beings indulged in grief, and that it was 'unnatural, and a barrier to continuance.' Perhaps I lost him when explaining how we are mistaken to live our lives in the shadow of death, and invent religions and erect pointless monuments; instead of responding to death by giving opportunities to others, and making 'monuments of procreation'. I tried not to focus on him any more as I continued, 'A dung-ball is rolled to be eaten and then is returned to dung and dust: action to action, dung to dust'. There were tangible stirrings in the auditorium. 'A dung-beetle is the agent of the rolling process, and not the product itself. Death is a dung-ball, a means to an ends, a way to roll on. All metamorphosis is generated by opportunity, and dying in the veld is a catalyst, never a catastrophe, and never final. Dying naturally – that is *opportunism*.'

I recall there being generous applause and healthy audience babble before questions were invited. My relative inexperience had pushed the lecture over the allotted time, so there was less opportunity for interrogation than planned. Some academics challenged the presentation's balance of science and interpretation, questioning my lack of evidence, and my responses probably satisfied few. The huddle of environmentalists in green T-shirts asked questions, more to show approval and be heard, than to enquire. And as the lecture hall was emptying, and I had just turned off and was closing my laptop, one last question came.'Are you free for tea now?'

We walk to my department passing, as Jo informs me, under the branches of some indigenous trees, that I often admire from my third floor office window, and in which cicadas congregate and sing.

'Num-num trees – *Carissa macrocarpa*, and also known as Amatungulu.' She beams. 'The berries make such lovely jam.'

'At first, we didn't know where to get tickets for your show,' Bertram interjects, releasing a need to contribute to the conversation, 'but then we phoned, and found out it was for free.'

For the first time it is me, and not Johanna the dutiful Mrs Hidebound, serving the tea. There are no rusks but a slightly lopsided chocolate cake left by a colleague iced with *Best wishes, Rana*, is deliciously home-made.

Before leaving us to pick up Sissie who is 'really finding herself', and Sonny who is 'becoming more of a man every time I look at him', Bertram tells me about the political expediencies that had forced them to leave the farm at terrifyingly short notice. He allows, even invites, Johanna to comment on much of what he says, and is clearly defeated by the loss of his 'every... *everything*'.

'Gabriel's my boy,' Bertram says of Sonny, 'he takes me up to here now,' raising the palm of his hand, salute-like to his forehead, in acknowledgement that his

137

step-son and I had a special connection. 'I'll put him –
Murume – in touch with you.'

Then he rises, squeezes his wife's shoulder
tenderly, rattles his car keys, and gives me an impulsive,
and clumsy, hug goodbye.

'Thank you for listening, Bert.'

Although it has become habit to wear them, Jo and I
remove our masks. I am interested to hear what she
thinks of the lecture, and ask, suspecting I will get little
more than glowing feedback and motherly
encouragement. She digs into, and rummages through
the pockets of, her large handbag, and produces a
meticulously-wrapped gift, plastered with pretty
stickers, with a card that reads: *Well done for getting so-
o-o far. With love, the Hidebounds.*

'I'm usually a fairly dry academic but these last
months have been–,' I search and settle for the easiest
description, 'different. Do you remember how I used to
rely on all those facts to keep our conversations going?'

We reminisce warmly. I apologise for the absence
of rusks. We laugh. I ask about Sonny.

'He's at boarding school here in the city. I don't
think I like it at all. I believe they bully him but Bertie
says it will make him tough. Everyone calls him
"Dungy" now. He enjoys the nickname but I prefer to
call him Gabriel.'

Then I refill the kettle as Jo begins pouring out her news of the past year. The move from the farm was 'quite something' and, she believes, 'it killed the old lady'.

'But at least the funeral was grand. It was in the big church here in the city. You know, the one with the highest steeple, and the clock that jumps and the hands that shake when the bells chime. I could've filled the place with flowers from the garden, Rana. And so many people came to pay their respects.'

'Yes,' I interject. 'On a quiet morning I can hear the bells from my apartment.'

'Time passes – people don't "pass". It's not the right word. It's a misnomer. They "are", and then they "aren't". That's all. Like the sunset on the farm. It's something, but then it's dark.'

'Yes, it's *opportuning*, Jo,' I add. 'And I have this lovely new note book to fill.'

A stirring marimba ringtone alerts Jo to the device in her bag. After a knowing 'Hello' and a 'yes' or two, she switches to video call, and hands me the phone.

'Hi, it's Dungy. Remember me?' His adolescent voice is breaking, and oscillates between hoarseness and squeakings.

'Murume!'

I see Jo receding towards the window of my spacious office and looking out. I have Murume to myself, and it is warming to see him again, and hear the glee in his cracking voice. We have little more than exclamatory pleasantries to exchange.

'Gotta go. Can't chat long – we don't wanna harm any dung-beetles!'

Chapter 32: Returning

There were spaces in their togetherness, and the winds of the savanna blew between them. They created together but instinct imposed no bond. Their rolling was a moving river between the banks of their needs. They scraped and danced together, but let each other be alone. They knew to separate the grass from the twigs in their dung-balls. Revolutions of the moon drifted into each other, and waxings and wanings continued, in opportunism, and the manure of the farm animals remained in plentiful oversupply throughout the seasons. But when the rainy spell ended, the farm quietened, and the animals were moved away, and no dung was left.

I was always Rollo, always rolling – or preparing to roll. Sometimes I felt merely months old, looking up at the balancing rocks, newly exploring the outcrops, searching for duiker droppings, and knowing to not scurry into cover down busy dassie burrows. There'd been warmer dawns and wintrier dusks, and rainier nights and drier days. I'd managed many moultings, and expanded easily into unworn exoskeletons. I'd feasted and fought and pheremoned. My ego diminished, but never as sharply as over the days when the dung dried, and no fresh faeces fell.

The curse of *kungufisiza* had shifted with time passing. Overthinking gave way to re-thinking, which helped as the changes came. Thunderstorms passed and perspectives transformed. I scurried from needing to always prove, to myself, that what I was doing was valid. I scuttled from insisting, to myself, that I was meant to always keep going. Persistence could be paused. And so, with six feet more firmly in the dung, I ceased to be upended by my own stubbornness. I learnt *how* to scurry, and *when* to scuttle, and whether to stay or roll. I fed on the satisfaction of not merely finishing a dung-ball but of knowing it would be a brood-ball, a chamber for another life. I understood that I was a male of many moults, a complex coprophage in the great bog of opportunism. It had taken many metamorphoses to become a developed dung-beetle of my dimensions. True wisdom is gained in stages, and sparingly. And too much wisdom may be worthless.

There is no best of all possible worlds. Mankind is not the measure of all things. Everything can change in the blink of a farmer's eye, or with the swish of a dog's tail – but only on the farm, because the bundu does not blink. On the outcrops, lizard necks may flicker, and duiker eyelids may flutter, but the savanna keeps constant watch. Rollo had seen the gaze of the veld, and how intense a glare it could be. Of the thousands of coprophagi kept in busyness by Bertram Hidebound, few knew of a life outside Dunghill Farm. With the departure of domestic dung, and the Milky Way not in the position to provide, there were hordes without sustenance, from beetles to bacteria, and from flies to feeders above, around, in, below and near the dung-heaps. When the dung droppings had desiccated and the piles had turned powdery, Rollo recognized that it was time to move on. And this time he would not be the fear-filled follower, the chance chaser, as he had so shakily been, pursuing Kumburukha. He would, for the last time inspirited by his dead sibling's gift of opportunism, go, in his instinctual awareness that the season of longer days had arrived, and fly fearlessly, emboldened and encouraged by his mate, further afield, and find faeces in the veld.

It was a cool, cloudless night, ideal for winging. Layla aired her antennae and scraped the dung-dust from her spurs. She opened her elytra, and unfolded and extended her hindwings, and hovered. With the Milky Way and me navigating, she soared in my supervision, and stretching our wings over gardens and outhouses and fireguards and farm roads, we glided in opportunism towards ordure in the outcrops.

Chapter 33: Human Revisiting

The female dung-beetle lays the *zai* in a broodball that is already rolled and shaped. If it develops and hatches, the creature will have ingested its protective surroundings, and will emerge as a life-form the dung-ball could never have foreseen. As any researcher does, I want my focus to have some relevance and meaning, and perhaps even expose something newly important and, if possible, become an inspiration for further investigation and interest. In less than a year, my work has shifted far from academia and veterinary research, but it remains essentially about moving manure. Where there is excrement, there is existentialism, and where there is deliberation, there is dung.

The homeland is going through sweeping changes. People are having to let go and make space for opportunity, but there is doubt, and fear and abuse are rampant. For my ideas, I have been admired and admonished, and encouraged and insulted. There have been invitations to share my insights, and threats to silence me. The media have labelled me a 'daring disciple of dung and destiny' and 'societal shit-stirrer', and much in between. Last week I received a message on my website: '*I believe in you. Murume (alias Dungy) xx*'.

As I turn into the school, passing between the decorative wrought-iron gateposts, and up the driveway along the security fence to the boarding hostel, I see the young man waiting, as we arranged. He stands, back to the establishment, like an outsider, some distance from his hostel. He has survived almost a year as a boarder at high school, and is elated to see me. I notice his lankiness and gawky way of scurrying towards me. He has taken off his mask to kiss me, and is handsome, with a fuzzy chin, and our familiarity is instantly as warm as it was when I left him standing at the opened gates of Dunghill Farm. Today he will be my navigator, and body guard. We have plans, uncoordinated, to re-visit the farm – it could be unsafe but it is our secret.

More potholes have formed on the farm dirt road, but there are no gates, or fences, so no stopping this time. The homestead security gates are mangled and lie rusting in the roadside bush. The front lawn is waist high in weeds, and the indigenous trees and plants in the garden are flourishing and choking the fancy, imported shrubs. The vegetable garden is overgrown, and paths and beds indistinguishable. The place is no longer a farm: the outhouses are featureless, there are no animals, and no smells of dung. There is an eerie stillness.

Murume takes my arm and we saunter in silence over the cracked-cement floor of the verandah, and past the stark white skulls hanging, untouched and unmoved, on the grey and brown-blotched walls. He is the guide and, it seems to me, an unfeeling witness to a life not treasured. I continue with him, ambling and absorbing, and without a note-book.

'Come,' his voice squeaks, and '*come*,' he repeats, the manly gruffness now controlled, as he leads me to, 'your place'. The wall I spent many hours perched on, has not crumbled any further, and we sit and reminisce, about the same things, differently remembered.

To check how they may not have changed, despite a recent veld fire, we decide to visit the rocky outcrops on the way back.

'Do you think it's possible to climb onto the big, round boulder balancing on top?' he asks. 'You could see the world from there.'

We are held up by a traditional procession of praising mourners, wailing as they move slowly along the underused and half-overgrown bundu road ahead. They separate, stomp the ground, then settle on a nearby open area of ancestral land on which to engage in their rituals.

I last attended such a funeral, when my grandmother passed away, as a young girl, and thought the proceedings ahead of us would be of more interest to

Murume than the sentimentality of the two of us scaling the rocky outcrops. The road is blocked, anyway. He listens, wide-eyed as before, to my explanation that the dead person's body takes on a new state while the soul continues. So there is no event or rite as grand or solemn that demands so much ceremony and so many people in attendance - and that inspirits so much dread. There are usually more than five different rites, such as for burial, purification, honour, reincarnation and appeasement, performed as much for the dead as for the well-being of those remaining alive. I found myself veering into lecture-mode again, but affectionately now, 'so people better understand that death is real. The rituals help them in the grieving process, and offer them a chance to engage and react – to do *something*. These customs offer structured activities in times of chaos.' The mourners had formed a neat circle, and are eulogizing. 'Then the living understand the death within the meaning of their beliefs. And they feel a sense of continuance.'

'So it makes opportunities for their families, and the next generations. Wow, it's amazing, and sort of complicated,' Murume remarks.

We watch for a while, mesmerized. Then he enquires about the bright blue and green robes they are wearing.

'Yes, it *is* complicated,' I agree, and explain that there are ongoing cultural changes, 'like metamorphoses, so some of their traditional elements have been dislodged, or replaced, in this case by Christian influences.'

Murume is studying the procedures. He seems engrossed, and then asks, 'Where are their children?'

'Oh, they stay away. If they see the dead body, it's believed they'll go blind.'

'We need to be heading back to the city,' Murume says, looking at the time on his phone. 'If I'm not back before the 18h00 roll call, I'll be punished.'

Driving back along the open highway, we are still chatting, more animatedly now, about dung-beetles and dogs, and dunking rusks and dinner roasts, and politics and parenting, and learning. Without slowing down, I turn the steering wheel a little to dodge some well-smeared roadkill.

'Rana, did you understand the funeral, what they were saying? Or singing?'

'They were chanting. Praising.'

He sat in stillness as we passed under the road sign pointing us towards the city.

'You seem interested, Murume.'

'Yes, I am. Mostly because I still have to prepare something for a talk in class tomorrow.'

'Ahh,' I chuckle knowingly. 'Before it was dung-beetles, now it's praise poetry. There's a notebook in the cubbyhole under the dashboard in front of you. Just dig around for a pen.'

He finds and opens the notebook, and reads the inscription: *Well done for getting s-o-o far. With love, the Hidebounds.*

'Okay, think of someone or something you want to praise.'

He pauses in thought, and smiling, suggests, 'A dung-beetle?'

'Perfect. Now say thank you to it.'

'Thank you, dung-beetle.' He is mimicking the tones heard at the funeral.

'What is its title?'

'Master of the Stables.'

'How does it look?'

'Shiny. A black-shelled insect.'

'From where?'

'You came from the rocky outcrops, your savanna home.' He is eulogizing.

'Say thanks, and congratulate – and keep reciting and repeating.'

149

'Thank you, dung-beetle. And well done. My family thanks you. You have rolled a great dung-ball.' Hand across chest, he knows how to play along.

'Describe it.'

'A mighty circle of straw and manure. To nourish you. And your mate, and your children.' Years of churchgoing are delightfully evident in his litany.

'Now praise someone associated.'

'Great Doctor Kuwiwirana Pindula-Howland, of the University of Animal Medicine.'

'Not any more...'

'My driver, as we cross over the mighty Mubundovi River bridge, I thank you. My teacher, you have done a great service.'

'Really?'

'My family thanks you. You came to Dunghill Farm, and we learned the work of the dung-beetle. And the moving of manure. You spoke to all of us.' His eloquence had grown to a crescendo. 'You showed us that life is more than just a sheep pellet splashed into a puddle of urine.'

'I did?'

'When the nights came, you went to the stables. And sat on the broken wall and filled your notebooks.

You studied those beetles. They rolled night after night. The dung-balls were for you, oh Female of Medicine. And week after week you watched. And you discovered– ', he delays, and then remembers, as his arms lower: '*opportunism.*'

'Well done, my Murume, oh wise one, man of the savanna.'

We laugh through the cool of the late afternoon, travel-intoxicated, on our private road-trip. The car windows are wound fully down, and my music is blaring. We are not singing along, we are eulogizing the phrases, and dramatizing the emotions in the lyrics, and giggling, and are too soon in time to deposit my navigator back in his uncomfortable, formative brood-chambers school dormitory for the six o'clock muster.

Chapter 34: Affirming

Each long day wanes, the Milky Way beams, the deep shadows lengthen... perhaps it is time to talk of seeking a newer world. A dry winter bushfire had swept across the savanna this side of the River Mubundovi, but around the rocky outcrops there was scant vegetation to sustain it, so the flames died in places, while the well-nourished blaze roared and moved on. Scattered patches of grass shoots, green and nutritious, revitalized the surrounds, and from the soot-encrusted trunks of singed trees, branches had erupted in bright, tender foliage. A hornless duiker doe limped around, eyes darting, ever on the alert for danger that might threaten her two offspring picking vigorously at fresh leaves nearby. There were no longer dassies peeking and dashing around, they too had moved on, and their former burrows were reduced to sockets of ashen silt. The balancing rocks of the outcrops remained in timeless poise, but the small ledge that had protected the developing Kumburukha had shifted little by little in the tropical rainstorms, then slid, and lay flattened. Around the stones of his birthplace, there was very little dung to roll, and certainly, for his mate Layla, inconceivably less than she had been accustomed to.

I'd created the ultimate dung-ball, and there was no chance of climbing to that height again. As Rollo, I'd left my progeny in poop, a dung dynasty, to find their own ways to keep rolling and brooding. Back in the bundu – where pursuance endures – there were still tasks to be tackled, droppings to discover, and dung-balls to build. But I'd found sense in smaller cycles, in denser dung-clusters, and in finer findings in the veld. The brood-walls of my ego had softened and receded. The Milky Way had guided me back to my birthplace, and I was striving to stay in sync with the savanna. With *kungufisiza* compacted, there remained no urge to seek dissimilitude or find fault where faeces were few and far between and dung threateningly thin on the ground. Duiker droppings were ever sought-after, delectable – but distant, and time after time, I was forced to fly far to feed. I still had all my claws, wings that worked, and alert antenna, to collect and craft dung. On each new expedition, however, unfolding my wings proved more arduous, my elytra rotated less energetically, and my legs were feebler in flight control. I fluttered from shrub to tree, from shade to shelter, enthusiasm ebbing and ideals obscure. I ate the morsels I could, and remained hungry. I took in damp dung, yet I dried out. Was it time to fold into my shell, into that last-casing scenario? What lay ahead seemed shadowed by the past, while the present was bound in a new and gentler stillness that began where I was paused.

The stillness stretched outwards from the outcrops, further than the defunct farm, across the River Mubundovi and farther into the human settlements where insects were imbibed and gave special powers, and were mimicked for opportunities in magic. The stillness reached over distances across rift valleys and jungles, to places where the women, having dined ceremoniously on dung-beetles, became more beautiful in their beetle-like plumpness. Bringing enlightenment, the stillness extended over great deserts and mountain ranges, as scarabs escorted the sun across the skies of the pyramidal balancing stones, granting rebirth and opportunism. And the stillness radiated further, in beetledoms where coprophagi were the devil's steed, the storm god, the fortune teller and the ghost bringer, and drinker of the blood of the human Redeemer himself. Where the sun shone, and the moon beamed, there was light, and opportunism, and Kumburukha was connected.

With time passing, he drifted to places Layla would not go. The further he ventured, the less she noticed his absence. One balmy night, in search of droppings, he buzzed over the young duikers, and soared above their mother with the scar on her rump. Kumburukha was ordure-oriented. He veered past the clumps of trees where the cicadas shrieked. Trailing the dung of some cattle straying near the river bank, he settled for a moment on the edge of a sandy savanna track, and readjusted. A trotting jackal pair approached, sniffed and nibbled, and scuffled as they crunched, and ripped thorax from abdomen.

Epilogue

Thank you dung of greatness we praise you

Highest saviour of the savanna

You came from the depths of beasts and birds to give life

To feed the hungry and protect those who grow to emerge

Oh mighty manure you have done this service

To the beetles that bless the earth with their labours

For we honour their rollings and the relaying of life

And because you were so we have become one

We give gratitude to yesterday and to what is past

That allows us each day to wake altered and alive

To stand and give thanks in the middle of a stillness that moves us

And those that stay rooted in the ground or go slowly or move swiftly

As duikers nibble and dassies dart and jackals prowl and pounce

And cicadas sing into the night and rocks balance through time

As humans are evolving to know that life has forgotten nobody

Thank you for the creation of the land that is metamorphosing always
Help us in the mighty savanna to see further than our knowledge reaches

To find outhouses and outcrops where all truths can meet

As the rivers flow to share what is on both sides of their banks

We praise the moon that changes and the stars that guide and the sun that warms

And the rains that wash and breezes that blow across the land
We thank you for your teachings and for your gifts of opportunism

Peace will come because a service has been done

And we rejoice in our thanks

And we understand in our stillness

Amen.

Made in the USA
Monee, IL
05 November 2021

81481913R00095